The Girl Who Howled at the Moon

1

Belarus, June 1941.

Ivan woke up early that morning to help his father gather firewood like he did every day, so that they could cook their breakfast. His brother Igor would always assist with this task, always stumbling along behind him. Ivan always felt that he could do this task all by himself, his brother Igor just kind of got in the way. He thought it is appropriate that his brother was named after the assistant of Dr. Frankenstein, sort of a malformed individual who didn't really contribute anything major to the world.

Ivan knew that he shouldn't be angry at his brother, because it wasn't his brother's fault that he was disfigured and disabled and walked with a limp, just like his namesake, for which he was frequently teased. During those times Ivan would reluctantly come to his defense, even though he always hated having to do so. He wished that he had a normal brother, not a brother who was sort of the mockery of the town.

"Wait up older brother, you are always running so fast ahead of me," Igor said shambling slowly behind.

Ivan slowed down, but he once again resented the fact that he had to slow down to keep pace with his brother, who was not just slow physically, but also slow mentally as well. He also had no doubt that having his brother tagging along all the time was probably girl repellent. Nobody wanted to date the guy who had a disfigured freak for a brother, although if he said anything to that affect his father would have scolded him and beaten him severely.

His father was always telling him he had to look out for his younger brother like that, because his younger brother didn't have anybody else in the world. That may be true, but it didn't mean that he resented it any less. Having to constantly take care of his brother, and constantly carrying him around was a burden to him, a burden that he wished that he could get rid of one of these days.

As Ivan was going out to gather the firewood with Igor that

was when he caught sight of her, it was Anastasia, by a wide margin the most attractive girl of his age in the entire village. They were just about the same age, more or less, and he had always had an overwhelming crush on her. Of course the other boys in the village would always say that she was way out of his league, and that nobody would want to be around him when he was just the poor son of a farmer and who had a disfigured imbecile for a brother.

"That pretty girl," Igor said, drooling in a disgusting manner all over himself.

"Do you always have to embarrass me like this," Ivan said looking at his brother like he was some disgusting creature from another planet. He was tempted to hit Igor or try to get him to go running home simply so that Anastasia wouldn't see him with his brother.

Anastasia began waving over in his general direction, and he waved back as Igor jumped up and down waving his hands as well, doing so in as unattractive of a manner as humanly possible.

"Could you possibly be more repellent," Ivan said, not wanting Anastasia to come over and see him with his idiot brother again, again drooling like an imbecile, like he typically was. "But come on we have a lot of firewood we have to gather."

Ivan led his brother into the forest where they could hopefully find the firewood that they sought, but he would have liked to have just stood around all day staring at Anastasia. In fact, as they were walking off, he couldn't help but turn and look back at her as discreetly as possible. He didn't know how it was even humanly possible for a single woman to be that attractive, with her perfect figure and long jet black hair, but his friends were right, she was the most eligible woman in the entire village, there is no way that she would want to have anything to do with the son of a farmer, especially with his brother tagging around all the time.

"Look brother I found a mouse," Igor said as he held up a mouse in his hand with a big stupid smile on his face, once again still drooling down his cheek.

"Good for you," Ivan said as his brother kept playing around with the mouse. He figured his brother would probably end up crushing the mouse like he did with the other mice he had found in the past, which would always upset him, which is exactly why they could never have a pet with him around.

Ivan couldn't help but look at his brother with disdain, and think that he was the most positively useless person on the planet, or at least in the village at any rate. It was a small village, and word got around fast when you had an imbecile for a brother, and everyone would end up wanting to avoid you so that they would also be able to avoid having to interact with him. Being the person with an idiot brother was certainly not the way to become popular in this town, or any other town for that matter he figured.

Ivan also figured that his father probably wanted him to bring his brother everywhere simply so that his parents would get a break from Igor and having to constantly watch him themselves all the time. The truth was that bringing Igor with him made the task of gathering firewood even more difficult, seeing as Igor didn't contribute to finding any, and he was actively a deterrent, seeing as Ivan had to stop constantly to make sure that Igor wasn't running off and getting lost or hurting himself.

"Brother the mouse is not moving anymore," Igor said as he held up the mouse, which as Ivan suspected had a snapped neck.

Ivan shook his head. He didn't know how to explain this to his brother for the umpteenth time, so he figured he would just lie to him and spare him his feelings.

"I am sure that the mouse is not broken, he is probably just sleeping, why don't you just put him somewhere so he can rest and you can come look for him later," Ivan said as Igor smiled his big stupid smile and threw the mouse into the forest, not even thinking that the mouse probably wouldn't enjoy being thrown, even if it had still been alive.

Ivan finished gathering up the firewood and then led his brother home, holding him by the hand the entire way. It would be nice if Igor could carry some of the firewood, because it wasn't easy carrying the firewood as well as having to hold onto Igor all the time, but he would be relieved when they finally got home and they could cook their breakfast.

"Mommy mommy, I saw a mouse," Igor said as he ran in through the door and hugged their mother Anna.

"Well that's wonderful dear, I hope that you had a lot of fun with the mouse," Anna said subtly rolling her eyes in Ivan's direction as a Ivan nodded in acknowledgment that Igor had killed yet another mouse without even realizing it. It was Anna who told Ivan that from now on he should just lie and tell Igor that the mouse was asleep, because otherwise he would find it too upsetting.

Anna put the firewood in the fire and began cooking their breakfast, which it seemed was getting more meager with each passing day. With the war looming on all fronts they knew that there was rationing going on pretty much throughout Europe and elsewhere in the world.

"Look at my boys, someday you will grow up to be big and strong like your father," said their father Dimitri as he smiled and grabbed Ivan by his bicep.

"Me too daddy," Igor said, as snot dripped down his face from his nose.

"I would grow up bigger and stronger faster if we had more to eat, but I understand the circumstances," Ivan said as his stomach rumbled.

They soon began eating their rather thin soup for breakfast, as that is all they could afford to have for breakfast at this time under the circumstances. Dinner was the main meal of the day, so they had to ration for the rest of the day, and they typically skipped lunch altogether.

"I want more," Igor said as he slammed his empty bowl down on the table.

Every day Igor said the same thing, and every day they had to try to explain to him that that was all they could have because there wasn't enough to go around. But Igor didn't understand abstract concepts like rationing or anything more complicated than the mice that he had seen, and sometimes the birds that he had seen, who unfortunately for the birds that he encountered ended up just like the mice that he encountered, more often than not. Although at least in that case the birds often were able to fly away from him before he could catch them and snap their necks.

Even the birds didn't want to be around Igor, Ivan thought to himself, and began smiling and suppressing laughter.

"What is so funny," Anna said knowing that look in Ivan's eyes.

"It's an inside joke, you wouldn't understand, you had to be there," Ivan said knowing full well that they would understand.

After they had finished their breakfast it was a typical day of doing chores on the farm, with Ivan having the additional added burden of responsibility for having to watch Igor to make sure that he didn't get in any type of trouble during the day. Once again Igor was pretty much useless for any type of physical or mental task.

Ivan felt horrible for even thinking it, but he thought about the Nazis, about how he had heard about how in Germany they take people like Ivan and they killed them because they are completely useless. He knew that it was wrong, but he couldn't help but think to himself occasionally that there was a perverted logic to it.

He always felt guilty for thinking it however. As much as Igor annoyed him, if they put Igor to death he knew that he would feel guilty and horrible about it. For better or worse it was his responsibility to watch out for his younger brother, and that is what he would just have to keep doing.

After a long day of backbreaking labor just to make the minimal amount of food needed for them to survive with what the state didn't take away to redistribute, he always ended up sleeping well most of the time. But that night he couldn't help but feel restless, he thought maybe because it was the night of the full moon.

He went to his window and he couldn't help but notice that the moon was especially bright and beautiful that night, lighting up the entire room. It was bright enough that you could actually read by it. But as he was looking out the window down the street that was when he saw an unexpected sight, it seemed to be Anastasia walking around the streets at night.

Ivan knew that it was a rather strange thing for a girl of her age to do. Although he was only in the beginning of his teenage years, he knew about the birds and the bees, and he also knew it was unfortunately not safe for a teenage girl of her beauty to be out on her own at night.

He thought that he should say something, but he wasn't exactly sure what he would say to her under the circumstances. What are you doing out tonight, lovely moon we are having, he thought he would say to her, realizing it was a stupid line.

Ivan had to admit that he wasn't that good at talking to women, and even worse at talking to girls his own age. He may not have had the social problems that his brother had to deal with, but in his own way he was a shy and withdrawn individual. Even when Igor wasn't around to make him feel more awkward than he had been already, approaching a girl and striking up a conversation with her was not something that he felt ready to do, in particular not a woman that he felt attracted to.

It wasn't that long ago he started to discover the feelings and urges a pretty face could do to him. But he always felt weird about masturbating when Igor was in the room. He wouldn't want to do it in an obvious way because then Igor would wonder what he was doing and would want to join in, making an awkward situation even more awkward, and then he would end up jerking off in public all the time, and his parents would probably end up assuming that he had learned it from him.

As he looked out the window, and as he saw Anastasia under the light of the full moon, he couldn't help but notice again that she seemed to be wandering off in the direction of the forest. He knew that he should stay put, he knew it was none of his business, but at the same time he couldn't resist the allure of following her into the woods. He had to know what she was up to or he would never be able to get to sleep without knowing.

Quietly he started to tiptoe towards the door, when all of the sudden Igor woke up.

"Hey big brother, what are you doing," Igor said as Ivan covered his mouth with his hand.

"I have to go to the outhouse, just stay here," Ivan said before he realized that every time he said that his brother naturally had to go to the bathroom as well.

Ivan walked out over to the outhouse has Igor followed shortly behind, but he actually didn't have to go to the bathroom, his intention was to follow Anastasia.

"Stay here brother, I will be back in a short while," Ivan said as he started walking off in the direction that he saw Anastasia go off in. Unfortunately Igor followed right behind him, still grinning and smiling. "Didn't you have to use the bathroom," Ivan said, annoyed that his brother was tagging along once again. He wished that he had never woken up Igor, because he always ends up ruining everything.

Ivan began walking towards the woods as Igor continued stumbling behind, once again slowing him up. He didn't want to lose Anastasia, but he also couldn't lose his brother, because then he would catch hell from his father if his brother ended up getting lost in the woods, which had happened on numerous occasions, and which would also bring up questions as to why they were going into the woods in the first place, questions he would rather not have to answer.

"Where are we going brother, are we going to see more mice," Igor said as he started hopping up and down getting all excited at the prospect that he might see another mouse, which he would probably end up killing and thinking that it had just gone to sleep. Ivan would think the fact that none of Igor's mice ever woke up should have told him something, but luckily Igor was too stupid to honestly understand the mature concept of death.

"Yes, we are going to see mice," Ivan said, lying to keep his brother following him. He would rather tell his brother to go back to the house, but he knew that his brother would get lost by himself, and then he would never figure out what Anastasia was doing in the forest.

Soon they came to a clearing in the woods where he could see Anastasia standing there, staring up at the full moon as though she were in a trance of some kind. Then she ended up doing the last thing in the world that he expected, the thing that he couldn't have imagined or wished for in his wildest dreams.

Anastasia slowly began slipping out of her clothing until she was standing there naked with her clothing in a pile at her feet. Ivan always knew that she was beautiful, but standing there completely naked, bathed only in the light of the moon, it was like an actual work of art, the type of thing that a painter from the Renaissance would paint. He felt that she was perfection made flesh.

"Are there any mice brother," Igor said before Ivan covered up his mouth.

"Igor I need you to be really really quiet right now, or else I'm going to bop you on the head, do you understand," Ivan said as Igor nodded, before he slowly removed his hand from his mouth.

That was when Igor saw exactly what he was looking at, and in this case his drooling was more than justified, because Ivan found himself drooling a little bit as well.

"She's real purdy, she's not wearing any clothes," Igor said with his big stupid smile, seeming bigger and stupider than usual, again entirely justified under the circumstances, as he was pretty sure that Igor had never seen a girl with her clothing off either.

"I told you to be quiet," Ivan said as he once again covered up Igor's mouth and put his finger over his lips, indicating for him to shush.

For a moment it seemed like Anastasia had stopped, as though she had known they were there. She looked around as though she thought she heard them, and maybe she had, which is the absolute last thing on earth that Ivan would want, as he didn't know how he would explain this to Anastasia, although in a moment, although he didn't realize it yet, soon he would see something that he thought that Anastasia would never be able to explain to him.

Anastasia continued looking up at the moon, standing there naked, when all of a sudden she started getting down on all fours and making what sounded like a low howling noise, like she was some type of animal.

"Is she a doggie?" Igor said as he laughed stupidly and clapped his hands briefly.

Ivan himself didn't know exactly what Anastasia was doing. Had she gone completely insane, or was she part of some type of secret pagan cult? He had never seen a girl outside naked like that before dancing under the full moon. He had heard about in the Middle Ages that was a sign that you are a practitioner of witchcraft, although his teacher told him that these were all superstitions from the Middle Ages, and that nobody in the modern rational world believed that anymore.

Ivan continued watching as though he were in a trance with her, as Anastasia continued making what sounded like howling noises that started to get louder and more distinctly animal like. She had her naked ass arched up high into the air as she continued crouching down on all fours and seemingly scratching the ground with her hands.

As he continued watching and Anastasia started twirling around in a circle, as though she were chasing her own rear end, he found himself reaching his hand into his pants and gripping his genitals in them and jerking slightly. However before he could go to completion that was when he saw the one thing that would probably be the defining moment of his life from then on, something that he would never be able to explain, and that shattered the rationalist worldview that his teachers had tried to instill in him from a young age.

Anastasia started to arch her back in what looked like a painful manner, and that was when Ivan took his hand out of his pants and realized that it seemed as though Anastasia had grown a tail, not only had she grown a tail but it seemed like her body, once completely naked, was now covered in a thin layer of fur. Ivan rubbed his eyes several times, because he couldn't believe what he was seeing, but it appeared as though Anastasia had just turned herself into a wolf right before his eyes.

Ivan and Igor stood there standing dumbfounded as they looked at the wolf that had once been Anastasia, as it let out an ear piercing howl at the moon before bolting off into the forest.

Igor let out a scream and began running, and soon Ivan began chasing him. Ivan felt that he was chasing his brother simply because he didn't want his brother to get lost, but he actually felt glad towards his brother for the first time ever, because for him to run away in fear meant that it was okay for Ivan to do likewise without it necessarily being obvious.

The two of them ran until they got home, and just when they were about to run in the door that was when Ivan grabbed Igor by the back of his shirt and looked him directly in the eye. "No matter what happens you can't tell anybody what we have seen here tonight, we didn't see Anastasia, we didn't see a naked girl, we didn't see a wolf and we most certainly didn't see a naked girl turn into a wolf, do you understand?"

Ivan knew that Igor was an idiot, but as he looked Igor in his glassy vacant stare of his eyes, he somehow knew that this time Igor knew that they had both witnessed something that even he realized was illogical, and that was not the type of thing that you would talk about if you wanted anybody to ever take you seriously.

Slowly and quietly they went back to the outhouse where they both relieved themselves in more senses of the word than one. Then they slowly crept back into their bedroom and got under the sheets, and Ivan knew that neither of them would be sleeping anymore for the rest of that night, and if he woke up in the morning still remembering what he had seen that night he didn't suspect he would be sleeping much for many nights to come, and that neither would Igor.

2

Ivan never fully fell asleep that night, but when he woke up the next morning, feeling the sun coming through the window onto his body, he felt safer now that the night had been chased away, the night and all of its weird goings on and its monsters and unexplained phenomenon.

"Maybe I had just imagined it," Ivan said to himself as he sat in bed, shaking his head. He didn't think it was that illogical to make such an assumption. What he saw was clearly impossible, and if it was impossible it made more sense that it was a dream. However he knew that he was fully awake when he had it, and he knew that he never fell asleep after he had witnessed it. No, in all honesty, that was probably the most vivid moment of awakeness of his entire life, even if it seemed like a dream at the time.

Ivan looked over in the bed next to him and he saw that Igor was still sitting in bed with a big stupid smile on his face, clearly having never fallen asleep himself.

"You saw it didn't you?" Ivan said as Igor nodded and continued drooling. Ivan was glad that at least Igor seemed like he was more excited than he was afraid, but he was still worried about what was going through Igor's head at that moment. Igor was never a very logical person to begin with, owing to his low intelligence, so maybe for him seeing someone turn into a wolf like that wasn't as much of a shattering of his worldview the way it was for Ivan. In fact maybe Igor didn't even realize that it wasn't normal for a girl to strip naked and turn into a wolf, but he thought that even Igor had that much basic common sense and rationality.

"Was she a monster," Igor finally said, as though anticipating what Ivan was thinking.

"No, she wasn't a monster," Ivan said not exactly sure how to answer that question. He loved Anastasia, so didn't want to see her as some type of unholy monster, and yet the evidence of his eyes suggested otherwise. The evidence of his eyes last night suggested that there was such a thing in the world as supernatural monsters that weren't subject to the rules of the rational world as he knew it, regardless of however beautiful and attractive that alleged monster happened to be.

"She was Purdy," Igor said as he smiled and continued drooling.

"That she was, but you can't say anything about this to anyone, you understand that? Not to mom, not to dad, not to her, not to anybody."

"Can I tell sister?"

"No you cannot tell sister!"

Ivan wasn't exactly sure what he was more worried about, that people would think that they were perverts for looking at a naked girl in the forest, or think that they were insane for saying that they saw a girl turn into a wolf. No matter what they did telling other people about this couldn't result in anything positive for them, so it was easier just to keep quiet about it for the time being.

Their parents came by to wake them up for breakfast and they went to have their meager rations once again.

"You boys looked tired, have trouble sleeping last night?" Dimitri asked.

"Well you know it's the full moon and sometimes that can make it hard to sleep," Ivan said as he slowly slurped his soup.

"We saw a wolf," Igor said getting all excited and clapping his hands as he suddenly stopped eating, which is something that he never did unless he was extremely excited, otherwise he would tend to stuff food into his mouth until he was practically choking or until there was none left to choke down.

"What, a wolf you say?" Dimitri said. "I didn't think we had any wolves right around here. Maybe I should put the traps out and try to catch the wolf, as we don't want it eating our chickens or anything like that, as we already have a severe lack of food as it is."

"No, I mean I don't think that's necessary," Ivan suddenly spoke up without thinking. "What I mean is that I don't think that the wolf is it going to be a problem or anything to worry about, we don't need to hurt the wolf or anything like that."

Dimitri shook his head. "A wolf is a dangerous animal; we can't have it going around eating our chickens or our livestock or threatening us."

Ivan didn't exactly consider Anastasia to be a deadly animal, and the thought of her getting stuck in some type of trap for animals was a terrifying thought to him. He didn't want Anastasia to end up finding herself injured because of some type of trap her father had set. What he didn't know at this time was that whether Anastasia controlled the wolf or had any memory of the wolf when she became the wolf. It's not as though he could just go up and ask her like he was talking about the weather or something more mundane like that.

"The wolf is really Purdy," Igor said with that big stupid,

Ivan would even go so far as to say horny, smile on his face.

"Yes wolves are very beautiful animals," Anna said. "But they are also very dangerous. If we have a wolf in the area we have to do something to stop it from interfering with our food supply."

"I will have to set up a trap outside of the chicken coop," Dimitri said.

The rest of them continued eating their soup without saying much. Ivan was kind of glad that Igor was still hungry enough that he was stuffing his face and wasn't saying anything more about what they had seen last night. Although even if he had said something like that Ivan would just play dumb and go along with it, as though he were humoring Igor, and their parents would probably dismiss anything that he had claimed to have seen as just his imagination.

Once they had finished their breakfast and cleared the table, Ivan and Igor began to do their daily chores while their father set up a trap outside of the chicken coop, hoping to catch the wolf.

"It's the Purdy wolf," Igor said smiling and pointing off in the distance.

"The wolf, where," Ivan said as he turned around and saw Anastasia coming their way. "It's Anastasia, Igor remember not to say anything about what we saw last night."

"She's really Purdy," Igor said as he started drooling again.

"Hi Ivan, hi Igor, how are you today," Anastasia said as she came by with a big smile on her face, real casual and everything, not as though she had just spent the last night prowling the woods naked as a wolf, perhaps hunting people like them for sport.

"Hi Anastasia, we are doing well, how are you today," Ivan said as he let out a big yawn as Igor did likewise.

"I guess you didn't sleep very well last night either did you," Anastasia said.

"I think it's the full moon, sometimes the full moon keeps me awake like that," Ivan said not wanting to say too much about the situation, not wanting to give away any hint that he knew more than he was letting on. When he had a secret like that he was trying to keep it made his social awkwardness even more severe than it normally was, the fact that she was actually talking to him all of the sudden only exacerbated the problem.

Anastasia nodded. "Yes I have found that to be true as well, I never seem to sleep very well the night of the full moon, I always wake up the next morning really tired, as though I had been out all night or something."

Ivan was trying to read between the lines, was Anastasia trying to admit something to him, trying to tell him that she was out all night as a wolf, or was he just jumping to conclusions? He always hated these types of situations where he wasn't sure exactly how to respond. Then again what type of response are you supposed to have when you are talking to a girl that you saw transform into a werewolf the night before?

"We saw a wolf," Igor said smiling and drooling as he looked at Anastasia, not even being subtle about the fact that he was looking between her cleavage.

"A wolf?" Anastasia said looking as though she were surprised. "I didn't think that we had any wolves around here."

"You didn't see the wolf then I guess," Ivan said, once again trying to see if she was going to let on more than she knew.

Anastasia shook her head. "I can't remember the last time I actually saw a wolf around here, I figured a lot of the hunters killed them off for food and for their furs. With food getting scarcer around here every day people are hunting whatever they can."

"Well yeah, my dad is going to put a trap out to catch the wolf if it tries to go after our chickens," Ivan said, suddenly not sure if he should have given her that information. Was it her trying to warn her about the trap? Did she even know she was a werewolf?

"Well that's probably for the best, as you can't be too careful with all of those dangerous things and creatures out there," Anastasia said. Was she referring to herself when she was talking about dangerous things and creatures?

"Yeah, you can never be too safe and all of that," Ivan said, not exactly sure where this conversation was going.

"Anyway I had better get back, as I am supposed to take care of my grandmother today and I don't want to keep her waiting, I hope you boys have a nice day and everything," Anastasia said smiling and skipping off.

"You too," Ivan said as she walked off and Igor continued staring at her and drooling.

"She's real Purdy," Igor repeated for the millionth time before Ivan bopped him on the head, causing him to rub his head. "What was that for?"

"Nothing, just be quiet and don't say anything, we have to go gather the firewood," Ivan said as he and Igor began their daily chore of collecting their firewood so that they would have more left to cook their dinner later.

For a long time they went into the woods looking for their firewood without saying anything. Maybe after bopping him on the head one Igor was finally ready to shut up. Ivan found it a refreshing change of pace not to have to be dealing with his brother's constant questions and babbling.

"Brother," Igor eventually said after a long stretch of silence.

"What is it brother?" Ivan said as he put down the firewood to rest for a moment.

"How did the Purdy girl turn into the wolf?"

"I don't know Igor, it shouldn't be possible, and yet somehow it is. I don't know how to explain it to you given that you are, you just wouldn't understand, you aren't old enough."

That was the nicest way he could tell Igor saying he was too much of an imbecile to comprehend any of this stuff. Although in fairness to him, Ivan didn't have any idea how this was possible either, so he was just as ignorant on the topic of werewolves as his brother was. Everything that he had ever been taught had told him that things like witches and vampires and werewolves were medieval superstitions created by the church to control people, totally out of line with today's modern rational society and the new society that people were trying to build.

Yet once again he couldn't deny what he had seen with his own eyes. He knew he wasn't hallucinating, Igor saw it too, and although Igor was a dimwit it didn't change the fact that he was also a witness. If only Igor hadn't seen the werewolf as well, then Ivan would have been able to dismiss it easily, if only he had just seen the werewolf he probably could have convinced himself with enough effort that he had been hallucinating, but the fact that they both watched the entire thing from start to finish and were still talking about it meant that they couldn't deny the reality of it.

The problem is he didn't know how he was supposed to get answers. He couldn't exactly ask Anastasia if she were a werewolf. If she had no idea she was a werewolf she would probably think he was crazy, and worse if she did know she was a werewolf he had no idea how she would respond to be outed like that. The way he thought it was pretty much a lose lose situation to ever bring the subject up with her.

Strangely enough he thought to himself that the idea of Anastasia being a werewolf almost made her more attractive in some way. He didn't know how exactly, but just something about the fact that she had that kind of power, well that made her even more mysterious and interesting than she was before.

"Look brother, wolf tracks," Igor said, interrupting Ivan's inner monologue as he pointed to the ground.

Ivan usually ignored most of what his brother said, but he couldn't deny that there were actually tracks in the ground. He figured it was probably just from last night, in fact as they were standing there in the field he realized this is exactly where they had been watching Anastasia as she made her astonishing transformation that defied all logic and rationality.

For a moment Ivan was tempted to follow those tracks, but not knowing where they would lead, and not wanting to have to deal with bringing Igor along to follow them, he knew that it was best just to leave this alone. The tracks were probably made by her last night and they probably weren't fresh. But the intriguing possibility that by following the footprints that maybe it could lead him to some answers was very hard to resist.

"Come on brother, let's get home so our parents won't worry about us," Ivan said, fighting his irresistible desire to try and figure out where those tracks led.

Later that evening when they were eating dinner, all Ivan could think about was Anastasia. He felt that Igor was probably thinking similar, but luckily by the end of the day he was more tired and tended to be quiet and hopefully would end up sleeping better that night. They had both slept poorly the night before, and they were hoping that they would end up getting a good night's sleep to make up for it.

One thing Ivan couldn't stop thinking about though was the fact that Anastasia was from that family of Gypsys. He knew that there was some association between Gypsies and the supernatural, but he had never probed into it that much, but he couldn't help but wonder if Anastasia being a werewolf had something to do with her Gypsy heritage, that maybe Gypsies knew more about these type of things.

"Well you boys can sleep soundly tonight, your father made sure to put that trap outside of the chicken coop, so if that wolf happens to come back we will catch the bastard," Anna said folding her arms and smiling smugly.

"Are you sure that was necessary?" Ivan asked, suddenly getting defensive over the idea of a trap.

"It is necessary if we don't want the wolf getting into our chicken coop and eating our limited food supplies," Dimitri said. "Don't worry about that wolf, if he's foolish enough to try and attack our chickens he will get what is coming for him, and if we do end up catching a wolf, well that's more food for us!"

As Dimitri laughed Ivan couldn't help but think that it was a sick thought to think that he could be actually eating Anastasia. What would happen if she did get stuck in the trap and it killed her, would she transform back into a naked girl, or would she remain in wolf form? These were more questions that he would rather not have his mind be troubled with.

That night as he went to sleep he couldn't help but constantly look out the window. Every time he heard something outside he would look to the trap to make sure that Anastasia wasn't somehow stuck inside of it. He felt like he was doing a silent vigil for her sake, to protect her from the mechanizations of her father who just wanted to protect his family's chickens from being eaten in a time of rationing.

He continued looking out the window again and again, but eventually, having lost already one night of sleep, he knew he wasn't going to lose another, and eventually, restlessly and gradually, he finally shut his eyes and went to sleep.

3

Ivan woke up the next morning with a loud yawning, and that was when he realized that he must have fallen asleep, and fallen asleep quite deeply at that. He felt a lot more rested and was thinking that maybe everything would look more normal today by the light of day.

As soon as he got up he looked out the window, and that was where he saw his family gathering around the chicken coop.

"Oh my God, Anastasia," Ivan said as he bolted up out of his bed, and before even getting dressed ran outside to join his family at the side of the chicken coop. "What happened, is everybody okay?"

"Well looks like we must have caught something last night, but whatever it was it looked like it gnawed its own leg off," Dimitri said pointing to the trap which was covered with blood and bits of fur and a severed paw. Ivan couldn't tell if they were from the body of a wolf simply by looking at them. "I am sure that wherever the wolf is now it will think twice again before deciding to try and eat our chickens."

"Do you think that the wolf is seriously hurt?" Ivan said, suddenly worried as his mind was assaulted with all sorts of disturbing images of Anastasia walking off holding a bloody stump for an arm.

Dimitri smiled and laughed. "I would reckon so, because any creature that would gnaw off its own arm to escape from a trap certainly isn't in a good position. Don't worry I am sure that if it was the wolf wherever it is now it's probably bleeding to death."

"Should I go look for it and see if I can find it?" Ivan asked, wanting to immediately start looking for Anastasia to make sure that she was not bleeding to death somewhere in the forest with a gnarled arm.

"But why would you even bother, it's just a wolf, if it dies it will end up dying wherever it goes, and if we find it later we can make use of the meat and the fur, but otherwise it's no big deal," Anna said.

Of course Ivan wasn't worrying about some lone stray wolf that was just straggling about, he was worried that the woman of his dreams was now bleeding to death somewhere and dying a slow and cruel death in the forest, but of course he wasn't about to tell his mother that.

"My young brother, it seems like in the last couple of days you have become overly obsessed with this wolf, like you are in love with the wolf or something," his sister Irena said. She didn't say much most of the time, but she always liked to joke about any romantic interest that her brother showed, human or otherwise.

"But the wolf is really Purdy," Igor said smiling wide again.

Irena shook her head. "Oh great it seems like both of my brothers are in love with a wolf, maybe you're going to have to start wearing wolfs bane as a way of keeping all the wolf girls away."

"I think I should go and look for the wolf," Ivan said.

"Come and eat your breakfast, as it's not much, but it's all we have," Anna said. "Besides you children have school today, you can go look for the wolf later, not that I think that it's a productive use of your time."

Ivan couldn't help but notice that his parents noticed that he wasn't eating as fast as normal, in fact he was eating more quickly than normal, but feeling a lot of indigestion as he pictured Anastasia injured and maimed. He just wanted to finish up his breakfast as soon as possible because all he could think about was the possibility of Anastasia being injured or possibly even dying somewhere.

He started to calm down as he thought that he would probably see her at school. He almost felt like running over to her house to check on her, but then he didn't really want to do that and then have to think of some excuse why he was in a panic to see if she was okay.

"Calm down, I am sure that Anastasia is fine, I'm sure as soon as I get to school I will see her and everything will be okay," Ivan said, trying to take deep breaths and get those images of Anastasia with her arm missing out of his head.

Why didn't he stay up later and make sure that nothing went into the trap? If anything had happened to her he would never forgive himself. Why did his father have to put out that trap in the first place? The chickens, were chickens really more valuable the lives of their neighbors?

Ivan started walking to school, and as he did so he was relieved to see Anastasia down the road.

"Anastasia, I'm so glad to see that you are okay," Ivan said catching his breath as he caught up to her, not able to hide the fact that he was obviously nervous.

Anastasia gave him a funny look and a sort of wry smile. "And why on earth wouldn't I be okay?"

Ivan found himself tongue-tied at that very moment, and decided that maybe he had better change the topic of conversation quickly before she started to suspect something was wrong.

"Well anyway Ivan, as I have you here I was wondering, do you want to go to the summer festival with me perhaps?"

It took Ivan a minute to process the words that he had just been told. Here he was panicking all about her possibly being dead somewhere, and now it seemed like out of the blue she was asking him to go to the summer festival to celebrate the end of the school year and the beginning of the summer season!

Now he knew he must be dreaming, a naked girl turning into a werewolf while he watches is one thing, but the girl of his dreams actually asking him out to go to the summer festival, now that was a dream for sure, in fact he was starting to think that everything from the last couple of days had been one extended dream sequence, and that maybe he was back at home suffering some type of major fever complete with hallucinations.

"Ivan did you hear me," Anastasia said, waving her hand in front of his face as he snapped out of it.

"Of course, I would love to go with you!" he eventually blurted out, realizing that he was probably blushing and giving away how excited he was.

"That's lovely, I hope that I will see you there nice and early in the evening, and we can have a good time of it," she said as the two of them began walking to class together.

Ivan was so overjoyed he didn't even know how to respond further. He thought that he should try to make some type of light conversation, but now he was feeling butterflies in his stomach, even more than usual, and this time not because he thought he was talking to a potential werewolf, but just because he was talking to a real pretty girl, or a real Purdy girl, as his brother would say.

"I can't believe that the school year is finally almost over," Ivan eventually said as she sort of nodded and smiled nervously. He wasn't really good at making small talk like this, particularly with a really attractive girl that he was gaga for, so he was wondering what they would talk about during the entirety of the summer festival, but he had at least a couple of days to worry about that now, right now we just wanted to get the class without his head exploding from excitement.

"My mom is very proud of me, as I got really good grades, she said that I exemplify all of the qualities of a modern day woman that she was hoping for," Anastasia said. "My grandmother is a little bit more old-fashioned and doesn't seem to think that this whole idea of the new modern woman that the communists are promoting is a good thing, but you know how old people are sometimes set in their ways."

"I got good grades as well," Ivan said, which was actually a pretty boldfaced lie, as he wasn't the greatest of students. He wasn't an imbecile like his brother, but he also wasn't going to be winning any awards or graduating as the valedictorian of his class, even in a small village like that.

"Really?" Anastasia said again with that same smile that said I don't quite believe you, probably because she had been in class with him all year long.

"Well, relatively speaking," Ivan said as the two of them laughed nervously.

"I like you Ivan, you always know how to make somebody laugh and know how to defuse the tension of any situation," Anastasia said still smiling, but now he was wondering whether she sensed that there was tension to the situation, which is the absolute last thing he wanted her to be thinking, as he thought he was playing it smooth and cool with her.

Anastasia was a very smart and cultured girl for someone who lived in a small village like that. That is always why he felt that she was out of his league, not just because he didn't want to admit that she was smarter than he was, and more attractive than he was, but also because she just had more potential than most people in that village, and a lot more potential than someone like Igor, obviously.

"I like the festival, the festival has lots of really Purdy colors," Igor said, annoyingly as a reminder of the fact that he was still there. Igor hadn't been saying anything while they had been walking, for which Ivan had been quite thankful, but now he remembered that if he was going to the festival with Anastasia he would get stuck dragging his brother around with them as well. Maybe he could convince Irena to take care of his brother for that evening, but he didn't want to admit it was because he wanted to go on a date with Anastasia, although that would be a lesser evil if it meant being able to go on the date of his dreams without having his drooling imbecile of a brother tagging along like some festering boil on parts of his anatomy that he would rather not be naming.

"Oh yes, I always like how they always decorate it with lots of flowers," Anastasia said. "It's even better than the spring festival, in all honesty. Summer is my favorite season, especially in a cold region of the world like this. Something about the renewal of life and everything just transforming like that."

"Transforming?" Ivan said, raising an eyebrow and wondering what she meant by that particular phrase, as though she meant transforming into a wolf.

Anastasia shook her head. "Just you know how the seasons transform from one to another, how we go from the winter to the spring and then finally to the summer. To me that's the most beautiful transformation in all of nature, the way nature just knows how to go from one thing to the other like that. Nature is amazing like that, isn't it?"

"Oh absolutely, that's of course what I thought you meant," Ivan said. "It's always lovely when the seasons transform."

Igor simply stood there drooling and nodding his chin. Ivan wasn't particularly fond of the fall because that's when Igor would pick up all the leaves, like they were something astonishing from another planet or something like that, and he would always ask the same idiot question he does every year about why the leaves change color like that, an explanation which would be entirely lost on his feeble intellect.

Anastasia nodded. "I have always respected nature, there's something about nature that it's its own special force, something primal about it. It was here before us and it will be here long after us."

Ivan simply nodded in agreement, he thought that that was actually a little dark, but he liked something about the fact that Anastasia was dark, and she might even be darker still, as she was actually a supernatural creature, which he suddenly remembered after that comment.

"My dad said that people are losing their connection with the earth, and losing their connection with nature," Ivan said, feeling that that was sort of a sophisticated sounding comment to make him sound like he was intellectually on par with her. "He said that when he was younger everybody was a farmer and was close to the earth and knew everything about living in harmony with nature, now we are sort of destroying everything, forcing nature back, killing off the animals, killing off the plants, destroying and overworking the land."

Anastasia was smiling large and wide now, and Ivan knew that whatever he was saying she was totally eating it up.

Anastasia nodded again. "I have always tried to keep a really close connection to the earth, which is why I often like to go for walks out in the wilderness by myself, even though a lot of people tell me it's not safe for a young lady to go out alone at night like that."

Ivan wanted to say that he knew that she was a big girl and that she could take care of herself, but that sounded almost patronizing. He also knew that as a killer werewolf she didn't really have much to fear from the world, and that the world would probably be more afraid of her than she was of it. But of course he certainly wasn't going to say that!

"I like going for walks out in nature as well," Ivan said, trying to maybe maneuver himself into going for a late night walk after the summer festival, his fears that she would turn into some type of monster and eat him be damned!

"Often I feel really connected to the animals and to nature in a way that a lot of people would probably find strange," Anastasia said.

"I wouldn't think that is strange at all," Ivan said as he shook his head. "I don't think that you're the least bit strange Anastasia."

Anastasia frowned, as he realized that he had said something wrong now. "Well I certainly hope that you find me a little bit strange, I don't want to be boring and ordinary."

"Well you're certainly a lot greater and more interesting than an ordinary girl in this village," he said feeling that that was a good save. He also meant it on two levels, she was extraordinary beautiful and she was also extraordinary because he didn't know any other girl who can turn herself into a wolf, that's a major talent by anybody's standards!

He thought he was doing good considering how socially awkward he usually was in a situation talking to a girl like that, but he was still much relieved when they finally arrived at the school and Igor went off for his special schooling as the rest of the students sat down in the classroom.

"Well students I can say I am honestly pleased with you this year, some more than others," said Prof. Sergi as he looked at Anastasia and smiled, before panning over to Ivan and sort of rolling his eyes, causing him to slump down into his seat a bit as the other students began laughing, including Anastasia, but it looked like it was more lighthearted laughter rather than the mocking kind.

The professor went back to give back all of their grades for the year and congratulated all of them, and saying to everybody how he hopes that they could get through the coming summer without any type of trouble. Once class was over Ivan knew that he wanted to stay behind and ask a question. He wanted to get home and walk home with Anastasia, but his questions were burning too much, and he felt that he had to ask.

"I'll catch up with you in a little while," Ivan said as Anastasia started walking home. As much as he wanted to walk home with her he had to admit he didn't really have any topics for conversation with her that he could think of off the top of his head, but he did have a question that he wanted to ask his professor.

"Class is dismissed for the year, it's strange that now you are hesitant to leave my class after you have spent so much time goofing off and playing hooky," Prof. Sergi said. "But I know that you are a hard worker Ivan, and I know that you have to do work on your parents farm, all things considered you're not such a bad student after all."

"Thanks professor, but I do have one question that I would kind of like to ask you."

The professor raised his eyebrow with suspicion and maybe a vague hint of annoyance as though he were as eager to get out of there as the students were. "Oh, you have a question now, now at the very end of the year? I wish you were more inquisitive the entire year the way you suddenly are right now."

"Well remember when you were talking to us about the medieval ages, and how people back then were superstitious, and that how superstition has no place in the modern world?"

He nodded. "Yes, that is something that they wanted us to emphasize in our curriculum, if we are going to be new men and women of the modern age we have to abandon our superstitions, all of these crazy folktales from the old country."

"Well you also said that every myth has sort of its basis in truth, do you think that there is any truth to the whole idea of werewolves?"

He figured he might as well forget about subtlety and go right for the information that he was seeking.

"Yes I remember that, but are you asking me do you think that I think werewolves are literally real? Of course not, they are just another one of a million medieval superstitions that have no relevance to the modern world. Oh sure I am sure that the myths were based on something, mankind has lived alongside animals such as wolves for generations, and wolves have always posed a threat to people, so the idea that people in the Middle Ages would be silly enough to believe that people could actually become wolves themselves, well maybe it's not so ludicrous from the point of people back then, but today people should know better. Does that answer your question?"

"Yes, thank you Prof. Sergi, have a nice summer and enjoy the summer festival," Ivan said as he got out of there as the professor waved goodbye to him.

He knew it was silly of him to ask his professor that question, as he knew what the response would be. No educated person in the village these days wanted to admit they believed in any type of medieval superstition. He didn't know why he asked him that, but maybe he was hoping that if his professor could able to entertain the idea of werewolves that he felt that he had permission to be a little irrational and believe in them as well, although it seemed less irrational when you witnessed it with your own two eyes.

By the time he had gotten home Anastasia had already gotten back to her home, but as he scarfed down what little he had for dinner that night he couldn't help it going to sleep in his bed finally relaxed, thinking to himself that dreams really do come true sometimes, but then so too could nightmares.

4

For the rest of the week after that Ivan found that he was practically floating on cloud nine. He still could hardly believe the fact that Anastasia had actually asked him out on a date, the actual girl of his dreams asking him to the biggest event of the season, he must have been the luckiest person in the world.

Although he was excited to be going to the summer festival with Anastasia, he purposely tried to avoid spending too much time encountering her in the meantime. He wanted to save up all of his conversation for the day of the festival, and he was trying to rehearse to himself what type of things he would like to talk about with her that she thought would make him sound sophisticated.

"You're going go see the Purdy girl aren't you," Igor would say each morning with that big stupid grin on his face. He had to admit that Igor may have been an idiot, but he thought that Igor was self-aware enough to realize that he had cause to be jealous.

Of course every time he saw Igor he thought to himself that he was going to be at the festival as well, and that he would be repellent to anyone, which is why he already decided to ask his sister to take care of Igor for the duration of the festival. She was happy to do it because it gave her plenty of opportunity to tease him about the fact that he actually had a girlfriend, but it was worth it to have the evening all to himself with Anastasia without having to have Igor tag along all night and ruin things by cramping his style.

At the same time he kept skirting around the issue that was naturally on his mind, and he had no doubt was probably on Igor's mind as well, even though he felt that Igor had a pretty short memory. Even someone with a short memory like Igor couldn't have forgotten the fact that they saw Anastasia strip naked and turn into a wolf right in front of their eyes like that, he figured that no one who witnessed something like that would ever forget something like that. But he still didn't know if Anastasia was aware that she herself was a werewolf.

She certainly did seem to be aware that she must have been a werewolf, because she had taken the time to strip naked right before she transformed into the wolf. But if she was aware she was a werewolf why didn't she mention anything to him? Hopefully she just didn't see him spying on her like that, but why did she suddenly show interest in him immediately after that?

For a moment he was getting nervous that maybe Anastasia, having found that he had learned her secret, was now going to take him off into the woods somewhere after the festival and then make him into her dinner as a way of keeping her secret forever and for all time.

"No way, she would never do that," he said dismissing the idea that Anastasia could be a vicious killer like that, although he had to admit to himself that although she might not be a killer, maybe in her wolf form she was a totally different person altogether, if she could even still be considered a person when she was a wolf.

He looked at himself in the mirror and he had to admit that he wasn't anything impressive. He wasn't a weakling or anything like that, but he also wasn't muscular the way a lot of guys in the village were. He was starting to doubt himself again and wondering what exactly Anastasia saw in him, which once again brought him back to the point that maybe all she saw in him was a potential for a quick meal, and then later they would find his body disemboweled in the forest.

That of course lead him to the next question that he didn't even want to vocalize but he found himself muttering in the mirror. "If she has been a werewolf her entire life, then how many people has she killed?"

He wasn't so naïve to believe that if somebody were a wolf like that or who had supernatural powers that they were entirely benign. He doubted that she just became a wolf so that she could go running through the woods with the other wolves, not that he could remember any time he had seen any wolves in the area other than her.

"Maybe the mythology is different," he said once again looking at himself in the mirror and poking his puny muscles. It was possible that just because someone was a werewolf didn't mean they had to be a vicious killer, even though in all of the legends werewolves were always seen as monsters and predators that were only there to prey upon the innocent.

In the end he decided that he would work up all of his courage and just suck things up and go along with it. If he really was a man he would be willing to face a woman, even if she was some kind of a monster. But could he really consider himself to be a true red-blooded man if he was terrified of a teenage girl, even if that teenage girl happened to be a werewolf?

He decided he would presume on her good nature, because if she was going to kill him or eat him she would probably just do it at night while he was sleeping, and he would likely never see it coming.

For a brief time he considered giving her wolfs bane just to see what would happen until he remembered that wolfs bane was poison, and that he didn't want to poison her of course, as that would certainly ruin their date and probably cancel any possibility of future ones.

"I'm going to make this the best night of my life and the best night of hers no matter what it takes," Ivan said as he gathered up a bunch of flowers from around the house, a good variety pack, none of which were poisonous, and hoped that she would appreciate it.

On the day of the summer festival, on the first day of

summer, the brightest night of the year, he was quick to be early to meet Anastasia. He tried to wear his festive best, and she was for her part wearing what looked like a Gypsy outfit from the old country, because he remembered that her grandmother was a Gypsy and she was probably doing it to please her grandmother, the traditionalist.

"Wow Anastasia you look lovelier than you usually do," Ivan said as he approached her carrying his flowers and almost dropping them in nervousness. "Although you look good all the time in all honesty, and I brought you some flowers, I'm pretty sure these only bloom in the summertime."

He had no idea if that was true, but he figured that it was the thought that counts right?

"Well thank you, this is a very lovely gesture," Anastasia said as she put them in a vase on the kitchen table. "How do they look, I think they look quite lovely there, don't you?"

Ivan nodded, he was just glad that she liked them, so at least he didn't mess that up.

"Look at my lovely Anastasia," her grandmother and her namesake Anastasia said. "It is so lovely to see you like that on this day of summer. You look as lovely as I did back when I was your age, if you can even believe that."

"I do believe it grandmother, and I thank you for the fact that I have inherited all of your best qualities," Anastasia said as she kissed her grandmother.

"Would you like me to read your palms," grandmother Anastasia said as she grabbed Ivan's hand. For some reason that made him nervous, he didn't have anything against Gypsies, but he always found something to be a little bit off-putting about the supernatural.

Did Anastasia's grandmother have any idea that her granddaughter was a werewolf? Maybe she was a werewolf too! Maybe the entire family were werewolves and they were preparing to eat him! But no, he wouldn't let himself give in to such paranoid fantasies, this was supposed to be the best night of his life and he wasn't going to let anything ruin that.

"I can see that you are a brave and conscientious young man," grandmother Anastasia said as she looked at Ivan's hand. Ivan couldn't help but feel that she was just trying to flatter him as she smiled, but then her smile sort of rapidly turned to a frown.

"Is something the matter grandmother?" Anastasia said.

"You are very brave, but sometimes bravery can lead to foolhardiness, so I will caution you to be a careful boy my lad," grandmother Anastasia said looking carefully at his lifeline. "You wouldn't want your lifeline to be cut short prematurely."

Now Ivan could feel his hands and the palms of his hands beginning to sweat, and he didn't want to seem like he was a coward, but something about that was unnerving.

"Grandmother please, you'll end up scaring him," Anastasia said with a laugh. "Come on Ivan, we don't want to be late to the summer festival."

"You kids go and have fun, but be careful, and be home before it's too late," grandmother Anastasia said, but she had a look in her eye that was extremely unnerving to Ivan still, and he was quite eager to get out of there in all honesty. "Enjoy your youth while you still can!" she shouted as the two of them got out of there.

"Don't mind my grandmother, sometimes she can be a little bit spooky," Anastasia said with a laugh. "It's important not to take anything she says too seriously, you know she's getting kind of old and her mind is probably going. Don't pay heed to anything that she said."

"Well maybe sometimes I can be a little bit foolhardy, but what was she talking about when she said stuff about my lifeline being cut short?" Ivan said.

Anastasia shrugged her shoulders. "Like I said, don't pay her any heed, today we shouldn't be worrying about our deaths, we should be worrying about enjoying our lives. She's probably just trying to say something cryptic to be all interesting and make conversation."

That was when Ivan found that he was actually rather relieved to find that this actually did provide a topic of conversation, because during the week while he was trying to think of things to talk about he was coming up pretty much blank. So as they walked over to the festival Anastasia told him about all of the superstitions that her grandmother told her from the old country.

"You see that's why I always want to be a more modern woman, I love my grandmother but she is so set in the past and the old ways," Anastasia said. "Not that there's anything wrong about the old ways and all of those old superstitions, I loved hearing about all of them growing up, with all of those things like vampires and werewolves."

"Did you say werewolves?" Ivan asked, his curiosity now definitely piqued. This was the first time she ever directly mentioned werewolves, was she trying to tell him something?

"Yeah but we all know that those are all just crazy superstitions and that nobody believes in those these days, come on let's go enjoy ourselves," Anastasia said as though she were trying to evade the question or regretting that she brought up the topic in the first place.

As they began dancing and eating and celebrating along with everybody else, Ivan's mind gradually started to relax a little bit more. If sophisticated people like Anastasia and his professor didn't believe in werewolves then maybe he shouldn't either. However he couldn't deny what he had seen with his own two eyes, and once again he found himself just as confused as ever to what Anastasia actually knew and what she was willing to tell if she did know.

"I want to go talk to some of my girlfriends for a little while, do you think I can catch up with you in a bit," Anastasia said.

"Sure, I don't want to feel like I'm smothering you or anything," Ivan said as he laughed.

"I would never feel smothered by you," Anastasia said as she kissed him on the cheek, causing him to practically faint right then and there, as she skipped off to see her friends from school who she immediately started giggling with. He was hoping that she wasn't laughing at him, or that if she was she meant it in a positive way.

Ivan found himself sort of sneaking off, and that was when he saw something, it was what looked like a Gypsy tent where you could get your fortune read. He knew that he was being silly and felt that he was giving into his superstition, and he didn't want Anastasia to see what he was doing, but he found himself creeping over into the tent and finding that inside was a Gypsy woman with what looked like some type of crystal ball. She really did seem like something out of a circus sideshow, but he if he was really there to get his fortune read then he was just as silly as she was.

"Do you read people's palms," Ivan said as he held out his palm to the Gypsy woman.

The Gypsy woman nodded and looked at his palm. "I can see that you are quite the ladies' man," she said laughing and seeming like she wasn't taking things very seriously, until she continued to trace her fingernail along one of the ridges in his hand before she stopped.

"What is it?" Ivan asked.

"Your lifeline," the Gypsy said shaking her head.

"What about it?"

"It's concerning, do you ever have a tendency to be a little bit foolhardy?"

That was the second person who read his palm and told him the same thing, and in the very same evening no less! He didn't want to believe in superstition but he had to admit that that was a little bit creepy, even for his taste.

"Well maybe sometimes I can be a little irresponsible and trying to prove myself in being brave and everything like that, but I don't think I take it too out of line," Ivan said suddenly feeling defensive.

"Ivan are you in here, I thought I saw you over here," Anastasia said seeing that he was getting his palm read and smiling. "This isn't because of what my grandmother said earlier was it?"

"Would the lovely lady like me to read her palm as well," the Gypsy woman said as she grabbed Anastasia's palm before throwing her hand away. "Please get out of here right now!"

Ivan looked at the Gypsy woman's face and she looked as though she had just seen the face of the devil, and he found himself swallowing deeply and his heart began to beat faster.

"Well she was certainly rude," Anastasia said as she grabbed Ivan by the hand, and he was hoping that she wouldn't be able to feel his pulse racing, because he didn't want her to think him a coward, she was the last person on earth that he wanted to think he was a coward.

"Anastasia, can I ask you something?" Ivan said.

"Of course you can, what was on your mind?"

"Did your grandmother ever read your palm, or has anyone ever read your palm before?"

Anastasia began laughing.

"What did I say that was so funny?" Ivan asked, now really feeling that he was making major social faux pas.

"Nothing, it is just that my grandmother always joked that I had the mark of the beast on my palm, and she said that she would tell me all about it but not before my 18th birthday. I never put much stock in what she said though of course, she's just a crazy old lady. You're not thinking that she is serious are you?"

"What, me, of course not," Ivan said pointing to himself and shaking his head and trying to do a convincing job of making it seem like he wasn't telling a boldfaced lie at the moment, even though that's exactly what he was doing, for which he felt bad about, as he never wanted to lie to her.

"My grandmother has all sorts of crazy notions, sometimes she is embarrassing, have you ever had a relative that sometimes you just have to roll your eyes and sort of humor them?"

"Actually –" Ivan began saying before they both burst out laughing as they both thought of Igor.

"You totally get what I mean then, sometimes you have relatives who are just a little bit touched in the head or out of it, and you just sort of have to humor them. Well I am sort of like with my grandmother the way you are with your brother, sometimes the best thing you can do is just laugh it off and try your best to enjoy life. Sort of like that whole phrase seize the day. I'm not going to worry how long I am going to live based on some of the lines in my hand, I'm going to live for today, and I'm going to live as best I can, to life!"

"You know that's a very good attitude to have, I totally agree with you on that," Ivan said as they both smiled and looked at each other right in the eye, and that was when Ivan knew that he had to do one of those bold foolhardy things that he had been warned against doing as he stuck out his hand. "Would you like to dance?"

Anastasia nodded and soon they were dancing until they were the center of everybody's attention in the village square, as all of the Gypsies began playing music and beating on instruments and shaking all sorts of exotic forms of music making devices.

When the two of them had finished dancing they both took a bow as everybody cheered, and that was when Ivan reached around and kissed Anastasia firmly on the lips.

For a moment he couldn't even believe what he had done, he was about to apologize, but then he figured that that would make him look like an idiot, an even bigger idiot than Igor even. He just hoped that his sister wouldn't hear about this, even though he was sure that she would and that she would never shut up about it.

The two of them continued dancing and eating and celebrating, and soon Ivan found himself forgetting all about lifelines and Gypsies and psychics and werewolves and all that other stuff, and realizing that he did just want to live for the moment, and right now at this moment his life couldn't possibly get any better, until that's when it did.

"Would you like to walk me home through the woods," Anastasia said as he took her hand and they began walking. They didn't say very much but just walking there under the moonlight on the bright summer night like that, he was just in paradise. He couldn't picture the night ending any more perfectly if he had planned every last detail himself.

At the end of the night they kissed again as Ivan escorted her home, and they said that they would see each other the next day, and hopefully every day after that for a while to come.

"So brother how was your little date," Irena said as soon as he got home.

"It was nice," he said struggling not to blush before he walked into his room and closed the door behind him and started jumping up for joy and pumping his fists into the air and clapping his hands.

"You saw the Purdy girl," Igor said, waking up in bed with that silly big stupid smile on his face once again.

"That I did my brother, that I did," Ivan said feeling good that he was probably making his brother jealous and feeling on top of the world. He knew he was going to sleep well that night from the exhaustion, or not at all from the excitement, but either way he was looking forward to it.

5

Ivan sat in his bed that night too excited to sleep. At first he was just waiting for his brother to go to bed so that he could masturbate to thoughts of Anastasia, but he found that he was too hyper and too wound up to possibly ever get to sleep after the night he had. It really had been the absolute best night of his life, and he didn't think that there was anything that could possibly ruin something like that.

"You know if my life could just stay the way it was right now, everything would just be perfect," Ivan said, although he knew life didn't usually work that way. He had one great night with

Anastasia, so he wasn't going to get ahead of himself and go assuming that it was all going to be perfect from here on out, but at the moment he was feeling pretty good about himself and pretty good about the world in general.

As he sat there in bed smugly satisfied with himself for the evening that he had, he put his hands behind his head underneath his pillow and thought to himself that he was feeling pretty relaxed. As he smelled the cool summer air coming in through the window he had to admit that he was feeling further invigorated. There was something about being with the perfect person for the perfect day that just made everything seem so much better, food tasted better, even the air smelled better.

That was when Ivan decided that he would go to the window and maybe go for a walk. Maybe if he went for a walk on such a nice night like he had with Anastasia just a few hours ago it would manage to calm him down enough that he could actually get to sleep, seeing as he knew he had a busy day on the farm in the morning, even though for all the farming he barely had anything more to eat than soup and potatoes. He was getting so sick of soup and potatoes, and yet at the moment he didn't even care about that, as long as he had Anastasia and everything else was going fine in his life he felt like he could put up with a diet that was almost exclusively soup and potatoes.

Ivan started walking, and that was when he noticed it, he didn't know if she saw him, but he definitely saw her, it was Anastasia, and she was also going out for a walk at night. For a moment he thought that maybe it was destiny, that maybe they were destined to meet up and go for another walk that might end in another late night kiss.

He started to feel a warm tingly feeling all throughout his body, particularly certain regions of his anatomy, at the possibility. He felt that he had to calm himself down though before he was even going to think about approaching Anastasia and asking if she wanted to go walking together, but then he saw her looking both ways to make sure she seemed like she was alone before she started walking off again.

Then he suddenly had a thought, a thought that he had completely forgotten about in the euphoria from the night before. The last time he saw her going for a walk by herself at night she had become a werewolf, although tonight wasn't the night of the full moon, so he figured that he was probably in the clear.

For a moment he almost felt like he had voyeuristic inclinations, as he slowly started following Anastasia without her knowing. Was he really hoping to catch another glimpse of her undressing in the woods and frolicking naked before becoming a werewolf?

At the moment he didn't know quite what he was expecting, but whatever it was he knew that he wanted to follow her and see what happened. He knew that she could take care of herself, and unlike most women in the village she wasn't afraid to go out on her own at night, wasn't afraid to be alone or by herself, she really was the modern ideal of an independent woman that was still rather uncommon in their small little, and in his opinion still somewhat backward, superstitious village.

Trying to trail slightly far behind so that she hopefully wouldn't see that she was being followed by him, he very subtly followed her through the woods. He could hear all sorts of creatures making noises in the moonlight, and for a moment he began to feel a creepy sensation. He had been out on his own many times that night before, albeit usually with his annoying brother tagging along, but something about leaving to follow Anastasia through the woods on this particular evening gave him a feeling of foreboding, like there was something in the air, but he couldn't quite place his finger on it.

After pausing for a moment to compose himself, he took a deep breath and decided to continue onward. He didn't know exactly what it was, but something was compelling him to follow Anastasia, something was taking him away from his home, and for some reason as he took one last look back at his home it suddenly seemed so much further away than it had before, and he didn't know quite why exactly.

He walked very silently, almost on tip toes, so as not to make any noise that would startle Anastasia. He wouldn't know how to explain himself if he was following her again like he had done that other night. He still didn't know if she knew that he had followed her that night, didn't know if she knew he knew her secret. In fact he didn't even know if she knew her own secret!

Maybe this time however he would get some answers. He didn't know what exactly he would do if Anastasia suddenly started stripping down and becoming a werewolf again, it's not like he was going to go up and greet her, but he figured he would decide on what he would do when it came down to that.

It didn't take long however for it to come down to exactly that. He had hidden himself carefully behind some bushes and peered between them with his eyes, and he could see that once again Anastasia was in the clearing where she was the other day.

"But tonight's not the full moon," he said silently to himself, as he rubbed his chin and continued watching. He found himself once again transfixed, as he slowly saw Anastasia stripping off in the middle of the woods like that, seemingly not the least bit embarrassed or self-conscious about the fact that people could potentially be watching her, not that she had good cause to think they were, even though he was.

Then he thought to himself who in the village would do something like that anyway? It's not like there were many other people out at night, well other than him of course, which made him feel like he was developing a new bad habit, even though this was only the second time he had done this, and both times it had been largely spontaneous and unexpected.

Once more Ivan found himself watching and trying not to drool as Anastasia got down on her hands and knees and began scraping at the ground and making low moaning howling noises. If she knew he was there he wondered if she had any idea how crazy she was driving him. He was beginning to feel like some type of sick pervert, or someone who was witnessing something that he shouldn't witness, and for a moment he was afraid that he would be stricken blind for some reason.

He thought he remembered something about that, an old superstition that if you spied on somebody undressing like that, particularly a beautiful young woman, you would be rendered blind. But then he thought to himself that that was another one of those crazy superstitions, although up until recently he would have said that werewolves themselves were crazy superstition, and yet here he was getting confirmation of what he had seen that other night.

He pinched himself several times, as he knew this time he was certainly not dreaming. He figured in a world where Anastasia actually wanted to spend time with him, even wanted to be his girlfriend, that anything was possible, even women transforming themselves into animals, in the most literal sense of the word.

Ivan continued staring as Anastasia completed her transformation until she was fully a wolf now and making a loud howling noise. For a moment he almost wanted to approach her, almost forgot about how weird the situation was, and how startling it would be if she suddenly found him. Of course as she was now a wolf he kind of wondered if she could smell him there.

Even as a wolf he had to admit that she was quite attractive, there was something incredibly majestic about her. But there was also something lonely about her, something about her alone standing there in the woods looking up at the moon and making low howling noises filled him with some sense of sadness, but at the same time he did not exactly feel sad for her, so much as sad for himself. As he watched her he knew that she really didn't need him in her life. He was glad that she wanted him in her life, but he felt that she really was in the truest sense of the word a lone wolf, and he wondered if they would ever be able to broach this topic, the topic of her dark secret.

Ivan continued staring at the wolf, and for a moment he was about to approach, when all of the sudden he found himself hearing the loudest booming noise that he had ever heard, despite the fact that there wasn't a single storm cloud in the sky that he could notice.

He knew that it was the sound of an explosion almost right away, but he wasn't sure what direction it was coming from. Anastasia's wolf took off immediately, not even seeming to care that she left her clothing far behind. As her wolf darted off into the forest he felt like he should be following after.

Ivan wasn't exactly sure what to do in a situation like this, but he did the first thing that came to mind and walked out into the clearing and picked up Anastasia's clothing. He wasn't sure if that was the right thing to do, what if she came back looking for her clothing later? But he felt like by holding onto it maybe he was protecting it for her, from what he didn't know exactly. But he just felt somehow safer over the fact that he had Anastasia's clothing that she had discarded in the middle of the forest like that.

As he heard the sound of more loud explosions, he looked up in the air and saw what looked like airplanes of some kind. He hadn't seen airplanes over his village like that before, so this was definitely something out of the ordinary, and something about it told him that he should be immediately getting home.

"We're being invaded!" he suddenly shouted to himself as a realization dawned upon him. Now his heart was racing, and for a moment even completely forgot that Anastasia, or what Anastasia had become at any rate, was out there somewhere scared and alone possibly.

However he knew that whether she was a girl or a wolf she knew how to take care of herself, and she was probably trying to return home just as he was. He began running as fast as his legs could carry him, stopping only every so often to catch his breath. He almost wished he were a wolf himself, because he didn't think that wolves got exhausted as easily as humans did, and he thought that they were faster, swift as a wolf was a phrase that he thought he remembered hearing at some point.

As he started running back towards his home, he saw what looked like clouds of smoke rising up and that caused him to stop right in his tracks. He didn't even need to complete his journey back to his village, as he could see from the distance that it was already on fire. He could see what looked like his home off in the distance with thick clouds of smoke, and he could hear what sounded like gunshots going off.

As soon as he heard that he knew that he should be running in the opposite direction and although he was out of breath he immediately began running away from his home, possibly forever, his sudden sense of foreboding earlier in the night suddenly making sense to him now. Maybe the Gypsies were right, maybe people can sense something in the air when something is about to go wrong.

He ran deep into the forest, trying to catch his breath as the sound of gunshots and explosions trailed not that far behind him. For a moment he actually grabbed his hand and looked at his palm.

"This is not the time to be foolhardy," he said tracing the lifeline with his fingernail. At that moment it occurred to him that he was probably going to die that night. It occurred to him that even if he didn't die right that moment he didn't have a home to go back to, that in all probability his family was already dead, victims of a sneak attack by a cowardly enemy in the middle of the night.

He could hear what sounded like more enemy forces approaching, so he quickly went and hid in the bushes and crouched down and tried to become as still and silent as a statue. He started thinking of his mother and sisters and then of his father, and finally of his poor brother Igor, who probably didn't even have the slightest idea what was going on, probably didn't even understand the concept of a war or even the concept of death.

For a moment he even felt sick to his stomach as he remembered what he had thought about his brother the other day, that it would be easier if someone had just exterminated him. He could feel the vomit welling up inside of his mouth, but he swallowed it and closed his eyes to suppress tears.

As he continued hiding in the bushes, his heart beating rapidly and his stomach beginning to turn even more, he could hear voices getting closer, voices that sounded German. He didn't speak German, but he knew the German accent, he always felt it was a rather harsh language and he didn't much like learning about it in school. He only knew a couple of basic German phrases, but he could recognize the language well enough.

The sound of gunshots and explosions continued, and the sound of screams also were echoing off in the distance, he wasn't sure what specific direction, but whatever direction it was he knew that he wanted to go in the opposite direction.

From his vantage point in the bushes he could make out what looked like jeeps, jeeps with the German swastikas on them, confirming his worst suspicion and fear, his country had indeed been invaded by the Germans, despite the fact that the Germans had supposedly signed a peace treaty with the Soviets, he remembered learning about that in his class, it was supposed to prevent war, supposed to prevent exactly what was happening at this very moment.

"I guess this proves you can't trust a fucking German," he said, realizing that that was the first time in a long time that he had cursed, as he did not make a habit of it, his parents didn't approve, although he felt that under the circumstances if there were any time to be cursing now was definitely the time.

Ivan wanted to be sick, but he continued to remain still until after the Germans had cleared out of the area as the sound of gunfire and explosions continued unabated in the background. He was not used to such loud noise in a small village like that, even the village festival, one of the loudest events of the season, sounded positively silent compared to this.

He never knew exactly what the sounds of war were like, and his father always told him that he hoped that he never would have to learn, but like so many in his village he knew that this day might have been coming, maybe not inevitably, but everyone had prepared for it, had prepared for the worst, or at least the possibility of it.

Until it was actually happening right before your eyes though it was hard to believe, just like it was hard to believe that now two times he had seen a woman transform into a wolf. That caused him to start thinking about Anastasia again, where had she run off to?

All things considered she might actually be safer in her wolf form. He didn't figure that the Germans would just shoot a wolf for no reason, but then on the other hand if they were just randomly killing villagers in his town why wouldn't they kill anything else that moves as well?

He didn't know exactly what he would say when he saw Anastasia again. Under the circumstances though the fact that she had transformed herself into a wolf two times now was almost inconsequential, considering that both of their families were probably already dead, and that they were now for all intents and purposes completely homeless in an occupied country, and who knows how long they could hide or where they could possibly hide?

Strangely enough, Ivan suddenly felt himself getting hungry. Who gets hungry in the middle of an invasion, especially after he had eaten so much the night before? Then again he had been running a lot and had been working up quite an appetite, but now was certainly no time for food. Not that he knew where he would be able to get food should he need any. All of his food was the rations that he had been eating with his family each day, and now he didn't have a home to go to, so he didn't know where his next meal would be coming from, which was always a source of anxiety, but at the moment seemed rather trivial.

He needed to find some way to survive in the moment if he was ever hoping that he would live long enough to even have to worry about food. He ran off further into the forest, not exactly sure which direction he was running in, or where he was going, but he just knew that wherever he was he wanted to get as far away as possible from wherever he happened to be at the moment.

Every so often he still had to stop to catch his breath, and he was beginning to become extremely thirsty from all of the running and huffing and puffing, but unfortunately he had nothing to drink. After running long enough he finally came to what looked like a small stream, and that was when he knew he had to have something to drink.

Normally he wouldn't drink straight from the stream like that, unfiltered water, but right now he didn't even care, as he knelt down and cupped the water in his hands and began drinking it rapidly as he continued catching his breath. Soon he was not even bothering to bring the water up to his mouth, he was just kneeling down and drinking it straight from the stream, like he were an animal, almost like a wolf himself.

As he slowly got up and wiped his mouth off he turned around, and that was when he saw the last thing in the world that he wanted to see, as he saw what looked like two German soldiers standing there pointing guns in his general direction. Instinctively he put his hands up as the two soldiers began laughing and saying something in German.

"I'll do whatever you, say but I don't speak German," Ivan said keeping his hands raised in the air. At that moment he felt like he was about to puke up all of the water that he just drank, as the realization dawned on him that he was probably a few seconds away from his own death, his lifeline on his palm didn't lie.

If he was going to die he wanted to die with some dignity, so as they stood there with their guns trained on him, his legs shaking with fear, he simply closed his eyes and prepared for what he felt was the inevitable, but as he stood there waiting for the final blow that would solve all of his problems, suddenly he heard loud screaming as he saw what looked like a wolf bite the soldier on the back of his neck before jumping onto the other soldier and biting off his face.

The soldiers dropped their guns on the floor as the wolf started attacking both of them. Ivan didn't even know how to fire a gun, but instinctively he picked up one of the guns of the soldiers, and as soon as the wolf was out of the way he opened fire, hitting both of them, until they fell down on the floor with blood gushing out of their guts.

As Ivan saw that he finally reached over to the side and began retching and vomiting up all the water that he had drank just a few moments before. He continued vomiting until he knew he had to compose himself and get out of there.

As he turned around to look at the two dead soldiers between them, that was when he made eye contact with the wolf, and he didn't know exactly how he knew, as to him all wolves had previously looked alike to him, but he could see from looking in its eyes that it was Anastasia, he was sure of it, and she was looking at him with that look of similar recognition that showed that she recognized him as well.

"Anastasia, I think this is yours, you dropped it," he said holding out her clothes to the wolf as he began laughing nervously, as he once again got down on his knees, held the clothing in his hands and began crying into them, as he felt his eyes burning from the smoke in the air and the thought of all of his friends and families back in the village, who almost certainly at that moment now dead, and under the circumstances he felt he was fully justified in doing so.

He didn't even care that Anastasia was watching.

6

Ivan couldn't help himself, once he started crying he began sobbing hysterically. He just couldn't believe that in an instant like that his life could go from perfect to a living hell, that everything that he knew and everything that he cared about, that everybody that he knew and that he cared about, were now dead in an instant like that.

Ivan continued sobbing into Anastasia's clothing until all of the sudden he felt a wet nose nuzzling up against his body and his face and something licking him. He looked into the eyes of the wolf and once again was reminded of the fact that he wasn't the only one in danger right then and there, Anastasia was as well. If it were just up to him he would think about laying down and just dying, but as he looked into her eyes he knew that he had to go on living for her sake.

Ivan took a deep breath and composed himself as he got up and continued wiping away his tears. The wolf made a low whimpering howling noise and started slowly scampering off, before turning around and looking at him. When Ivan could see that she was leading him somewhere he decided that he would do well to follow her lead, as she probably knew the forest even better than he did.

Once again Ivan began running, stopping only occasionally to catch his breath. Anastasia slowed down so that he could keep pace with her, but she still looked anxious to continue running, as she knew the danger they were in. He thought that she probably had less to worry about, seeing as the Nazis were probably not on the lookout for a wolf, they were probably only on the lookout for people, people like him who had managed to escape from the village by cover of night, and who now were probably wanted fugitives.

Anastasia continued running through the forest before all of the sudden she came to a stop and began growling towards the bushes. She quickly took off in the opposite direction and Ivan followed her and quickly dove into the bushes and crouched down next to her.

Through the bushes Ivan could see more German soldiers walking around with guns. As he saw the German soldiers holding their guns, which was when he thought what an idiot he was for having left those guns behind after he had shot those soldiers. As the memory of fighting those soldiers and killing them came back to him he was once again feeling his stomach turning.

He realized what an ignorant step it was to throw the guns down, even if the guns didn't have all that much ammunition in them. At least with a gun he would have had a chance against the soldiers, but now he was completely defenseless, he didn't even have so much as a knife with him. He had a knife back in his home, but little good that did him right now, as it was probably at the bottom of a pile of ashes.

Ivan couldn't understand what the German soldiers were saying, but from the way they were motioning it looked like they were sending out search parties in all directions looking for survivors. He had no doubt if they ended up catching him that he would almost assuredly be killed. What would happen to Anastasia he didn't really know, but he knew that Anastasia probably wouldn't leave him defenseless; he knew that she would most likely save his life once again, but he didn't want to put her at risk like that.

It felt weird the fact that he was crouching down inches away from a wolf. Normally he wouldn't get that close to a wolf for fear that the wolf would be attacking him, but the fact that he knew this wolf was Anastasia, that in and of itself was once again causing his head to spin.

In the course of just a couple of days he has witnessed the village girl that he was in love with turning into a wolf, and now they were crouching down in the forest trying to survive being attacked by Nazi soldiers from Germany. He was wondering what else could possibly happen next?

He figured that the German soldiers probably realized that he had killed two of their own not that far away. They probably knew that there was somebody who was armed, but the fact is he actually wasn't armed, so not only were they making a false assumption; they were making a false assumption that could endanger his life. At least if he had those weapons he would have been able to defend himself, but now they were out there looking for him, and he was completely unarmed.

The German soldiers started going in the other direction, but then a couple of other German soldiers came back holding what looked like trained dogs that were barking loudly. He could hear Anastasia growling loudly but not wanting to growl directly back. She was outnumbered 2 to 1, and the soldiers also had guns, so their best strategy was to lay low.

Unfortunately the dogs caught their scent, and they were soon going over in their direction. Ivan wasn't exactly sure what to do, but before he could think of anything Anastasia jumped out and started attacking the other dogs and frightening them off before she started attacking the German soldiers. He was impressed with how quickly her wolf managed to take them down, she was quite the fierce fighter.

One of the soldiers dropped his gun, it was just a small pistol in this instance, but Ivan dove out of the bushes, grabbed it and quickly used it to fire into the two German soldiers. He struggled to fight back the urge to vomit and managed to choke back his vomit into his throat with some difficulty.

Anastasia started making a low moaning howling noise, and indicated for him to follow her, as he continued to do so. They knew that there would be more soldiers looking for them soon, so he was hoping that she had a good hiding place, because he didn't think that he could go on running much longer. Having had nothing to eat in several hours and nothing to drink but water from the stream, and having vomited almost everything that was in his stomach up, he was already starting to feel weak.

He continued to follow Anastasia until she brought him to what looked like an opening of a cave and indicated that he should follow her inside. Inside the cave it was dark, and he couldn't see anything, but at least if he couldn't see anything, then neither could the soldiers that were pursuing them.

He could no longer see Anastasia, but he knew that she was in there with him, and that made him feel safe and not quite so alone. He was more concerned with her than he was with himself, although once again she had amply demonstrated the fact that she was probably more capable of taking care of herself under the circumstances than he was.

For the longest time Ivan stayed crouching down in the cave, and eventually he sat down, until the sound of gunshots and explosions off in the distance grew fainter and fainter until he could hear nothing else. He wasn't sure what to say under the circumstances, but he figured that the best thing he could do was to just stay there in the cave, because as long as they were in there he felt safe and protected.

"Ivan," Anastasia's voice finally said, after a stretch of time that could have very well been an eternity.

"Yes," Ivan said not sure what exactly else he would could say under the circumstances.

"I think you have something that belongs to me," she said, and for a moment he didn't know what she was talking about, until it suddenly occurred to him that she was in there in the cave with him, completely naked. He couldn't see her of course, because it was too dark, but just the thought that he was in the cave with her naked suddenly made him feel self-conscious, and he knew that he was probably blushing, albeit in the dark.

"Oh right," Ivan said as he held out her clothing and she felt her way around the cave until she was touching him with her hands and grabbed her clothing. Even though she was only inches away, he still could not see her because of the darkness in the cave.

As Anastasia took her clothing and Ivan could hear her putting it on, he stood there with his back facing towards her. Even though he couldn't see anything, he felt that it was only polite not to look while she was getting dressed, even though he had already looked twice while she was getting undressed, which she was almost certainly aware of at this point.

"Ivan," Anastasia said when she was finishing getting dressed.

"Yes," he said, still not exactly sure what to say under the circumstances.

"Thank you," she said as she leaned forward and kissed him on the cheek.

As strange as it sounded under the circumstances, they didn't feel they had anything more to say to each other at the moment, perhaps everything that had already happened spoke for itself, and there was nothing that either of them could say that would make the situation any less weird or any less tragic.

So for the next couple of hours they sat in the cave in silence and eventually, in spite of everything, perhaps out of sheer exhaustion, Ivan eventually closed his eyes and fell asleep.

7

Ivan didn't know how long he had been sleeping; his sleep at any rate was entirely dreamless. When he woke up he found himself powerfully hungry and powerfully thirsty, his stomach roaring and his mouth incredibly dry. He could see some sunlight poking in through the cave entrance, and that was when he remembered everything that happened the night before, it all came flooding back to him, and he found his eyes watering again, but he wiped them away and tried his best to compose himself.

"This is no time to feel sorry for yourself, if father were here he would tell me that I have to be strong for Igor," Ivan said before his eyes welled up with tears as he thought of the fact that his brother, along with his father, mother, sister, and probably everyone else he knew, was no longer among the world of the living.

Ivan put his hands over his face and was unable to stop himself from sobbing. He wasn't sure if he was sorry for his family and friends more or for himself. At the moment he wasn't quite thankful to be alive the way he thought he would be, and for a moment he wondered what he even had to live for, why was he spared when everybody else wasn't.

As he continued sobbing that was when he remembered Anastasia, and he started looking around the cave.

"Anastasia," he shouted, but not too loudly, in case somebody there was there to hear him that he wouldn't want to be heard by.

As he looked at the mouth of the cave, which was when he saw the wolf that he knew was Anastasia come to the entrance of the cave. Their eyes made contact and he quickly wiped his arm on his sleeve, as he didn't want to be seen crying in front of her, the fact that she was a wolf not making much of a difference to him at the moment.

Then Anastasia did something that was unexpected. At the mouth of the cave she slowly stepped inside and started arching her back again, and in what looked like one painful moment the fur retreated from her body, as did her tail, and soon she was crouching there with her naked ass up in the air.

She made a loud agonizing scream, as it seemed like her body was snapping back into place, as though all the bones and muscles in her body were a rubber band that were now snapping back painfully, and it didn't look like it was very pleasant.

Ivan quickly covered his eyes out of politeness, and partially a little bit he had to admit out of squeamishness. She had looked quite beautiful of course, but seeing her body snapped back into place so violently after her transformation was not something that was pleasant to watch, it was painful.

"It's okay Ivan, under the circumstances it is hardly a time to be bashful," she said as he uncovered his eyes and found her walking over to her pile of clothing and getting dressed. "Besides I think that you have already seen me before, and it's dark in here besides."

It was true that in the darkness of the cave he could barely make out her naked figure, but that was when Ivan suddenly felt embarrassed over the fact that Anastasia had known that he had been peeping at her. But at least now she had answered the question that he had wondered for the longest time, whether she knew she was a werewolf, and whether she knew he knew that she was a werewolf.

Anastasia came over and sat down next to him as the two of them stared at the mouth of the cave with the small ray of sunlight illuminating the entrance.

Once again for the longest time neither of them said anything. Maybe they were both in a state of shock over everything that had happened, it was a lot to take in, especially for him, at least she already knew that she was a werewolf, but he knew that she was dealing with the same emotions right now that he was, fear, grief, and apprehension about what was going to happen in the future, but at the moment it didn't seem like it was necessary to talk about that.

"I knew the first time," Anastasia eventually said.

"Knew what the first time?"

"I knew that you were following me the first time I transformed, not right away, but I could smell you in the air once I had transformed."

"I'm sorry," Ivan said feeling terrible about what he had done.

"Don't be, you had no idea what you were going to expect, under the circumstances I have to say you responded quite well, that's kind of what made me interested in you."

"Really?"

Anastasia nodded. "When you followed me in the woods that day and watched me transform for the first time, that's when I knew there was something different about you."

"You mean that I was a pervert."

Anastasia laughed. "I'm sorry I didn't mean to laugh, I was not laughing at you. No I don't think that you were a pervert, you just did what came natural, you saw a woman suddenly start undressing in the middle of the woods, I think that any teenage boy your age would probably have done exactly the same thing. However I feel that the average teenage boy, if they watched the full transformation probably, would have turned tail and ran out of there as fast as possible or even fainted. But you didn't, and that's how I knew you were different, and I guess having watched me transform several times now you have realized that I am quite different as well."

He actually did run, but only after Igor had done so, most probably would have left the second she began transforming.

"Well I always knew there was something special about you, I never would have guessed though that it was that you were a werewolf, is that the correct term for what you are?"

"That seems to be the term that fits the best. I hope you don't think that I am a monster or a freak because of what I am."

Ivan shook his head. "No, I certainly don't think you are a monster, I mean as long as you don't plan on eating me." He laughed nervously and she laughed back.

"Sorry I don't mean to laugh; it's just sort of nerve-racking. But no, I can promise you that I have never eaten anybody, the most

I have eaten has been small animals, and usually I wake up with a case of indigestion the next morning. In fact the first time I have attacked any human was just tonight, or last night rather, which under the circumstances I think was strictly justifiable self-defense."

"Thank you by the way, if it weren't for you I would be dead right now, I just wish that I had picked up the guns the first time and carried them with me. All that I've got is this pistol, and I think it only has one clip of ammunition. I sort of sat by the cave entrance holding it until I eventually fell asleep. I guess I am lucky that you were there to keep patrol, you probably kept watch on me all night long, I guess I owe you my life really."

"You don't owe me anything, I know you would do the same for me, you pretty much did last night."

Ivan smiled. "Anastasia, can I ask you something?"

"I'm guessing that you probably a lot of questions, but I think that I will get the first one out of the way by telling you that I don't know."

"What do you mean you don't know?"

"You're going to ask me how I transform into the wolf weren't you. Well the simple answer is I don't know. I mean I know how to transform into the wolf, but I don't know how it is possible. In fact for a couple of years I thought that I was crazy. Starting when I hit puberty all of the sudden I just found myself occasionally waking up outside naked, or waking up in my bed naked, with no memory of what had happened the night before, my clothing in a pile next to me on my bed or the floor and me having all of these weird dreams of myself running through the forest chasing small animals, and then I would normally wake up feeling a powerful sense of indigestion and often get sick."

"So you mean that it just started happening without explanation one day, just out of the blue like that?"

Anastasia nodded. "Believe me I was just as shocked as you are probably hearing this, but to actually live it I can't really explain, I can't really describe what it's like. Over time I came to understand that the wolf was part of me, came to accept it, now we are sort of one, I guess you would say. She's a part of me and I'm a part of her."

"So you remember everything that you do as the wolf and you control the wolf and everything?"

She nodded again. "I have control over the wolf to a limited degree, but sometimes when I am in wolf form my animal instincts take over. And sometimes the wolf has plans of its own. You probably thought that it only happened during the full moon, and while it's true that during the full moon I almost inevitably become the wolf, it's not the exclusive and only time that I transform. Like those two times in the woods, last night and that first night when you saw me, sometimes I just get a compelling urge that I know the wolf wants to come out. I don't know how to explain it, it's like just sort of a gut instinct, or some type of primal urge."

"So when the wolf wants to come out you basically just let her?"

"I guess you could say something like that, yes. It is pretty much futile to argue with her, so I concede to her wishes and let her have her time."

"So every so often you just wake up with this strange urge to go walk out into the forest, you strip naked and transform into the wolf, let the wolf do her thing and then when it's over you come back, get dressed and go back home and go to sleep like nothing strange had happened?"

"I know that sounds weird, but yes, that's more or less what I have done. As you can imagine I haven't really gone around telling anybody about this, but once I realized what was going on I guess I just sort of adapted to it. Everyone has weird things in their life, and I guess this is mine."

"But that's significantly weirder than most. I mean I have been sleepwalking a couple of times before, but I was never found naked or woke up with memories of going around as a wolf eating small animals. But I guess I can understand where you're coming from on that, you have a sudden urge to do something and that you don't have any control over it, but it seems like you have pretty good control over the wolf, I mean judging by the way you handled yourself last night. This is big Anastasia, I mean what you do, what you are, it sort of defies the rules of, well the rules of reality I guess."

"Like I said, I don't claim to understand it any better than you do. All I just knew was that one day I was a normal girl and the next thing I know I was wolf girl, going out for late-night strolls in the forest, getting naked and turning into an animal. And then sometimes I would come to this cave, which is how I knew where to find it, I knew it's a safe place and that nobody is going to find us here. I guess when it has been part of your life for long enough you just sort of get used to it, no matter how weird and unusual and inexplicable it is. Under the circumstances though you are taking it rather well, so I guess I was right about you, you are not like most people, and I mean that in a good way."

"So you really don't think that I am a pervert?"

She shook her head. "As long as you don't think I am a monster."

There was a long stretch of silence after that, neither of them sure what exactly to say next. What do you say when a girl casually tells you that one day she just woke up and found that she wasn't fully human, that she was maybe somehow beyond human. She wasn't just this new modern woman; she might have been a new stage in the whole evolution of the human race for all he knew.

"Anastasia," he finally said.

"Yes Ivan?"

"So what do we do now?"

After another long pause she finally looked at the entrance of the cave, put her arm around his shoulder and smiled. "I don't know about you, but I say that we survive."

And although he didn't know exactly how they were going to do it, all Ivan could do at that moment was nod in agreement, and for that moment it was enough.

8

Ivan and Anastasia didn't take long to start trying to make their cave a home away from home. They didn't really have all that much, basically all they had were the clothes on their backs and a small German pistol with one clip of ammunition. Ivan was hoping that he would never have to use that gun again, and that if he did he hoped that he would be able to make sure that he didn't miss the first time, and that he would be able to obtain a better weapon in the process.

Anastasia had known the cave from having been there numerous times before. She had been there many times in her wolf form, and there was something that her wolf seemed to particularly like about the cave, maybe the fact that it was well hidden and a place of peace and quiet out there in the majesty of nature. But she found that whenever she transformed into the wolf she ended up coming to this cave, which is exactly how she knew right where to go. In fact the cave had already been like a second home to her, she knew it front and back, like the back of her hand, or paw, as the case may be.

Ivan had to admit that the cave with rather musty and cold, and he didn't look forward to the idea of making it his own permanent home. He missed his own warm bed and his room, even though his brother often kept him awake at night with all of his babbling and moaning.

However Ivan thanked his lucky stars that at least he had Anastasia, as she was pretty much the only good thing in his life right now, and probably the only person that he knew who was still alive. As far as he was concerned from there on out it was just the two of them against the world, and he had to admit he sometimes felt inadequate compared to her, seeing as she had a special power that he did not.

All things considered he took it surprisingly casually the fact that he was now living in a cave with a werewolf, but he figured that if Anastasia, who actually was a werewolf, was able to get used to it, that he would find it just as easy to get used to, if not more so.

In fact he didn't even care so much that she was a werewolf, now that he knew that she wasn't going to eat him he actually thought that it was pretty cool, something that just made her more interesting. Still he felt that maybe he was accepting it as normal rather fast. However considering everything that happened in the last few days a girl turning into a wolf like that might not be the most earth shattering thing that had happened. Sure there was the complete destruction of your rationalist worldview, but on the other hand there was the much worse reality of having your family and friends slaughtered and your homes burned to the ground.

"Do you really think that we will be safe here for long," Ivan said, still carefully watching the entrance to the cave and always holding his pistol not very far away.

Anastasia shook her head. "As far as the Germans know we are probably considered to be dead, along with everybody else in the village. All the people we have encountered are dead, so they would probably just assume that it was random survivors. I don't think anyone is specifically looking for us, but I don't know if we will be able to stay here in the long run. Eventually the Germans will probably come and find this cave and start thinking that maybe partisans had survived here. At any rate I should probably be the one to get us food."

"You know how to get us food?" Ivan said, as he realized his stomach was growling, as he had not eaten anything in nearly 24 hours now, and he had thrown up what he had eaten yesterday. His stomach was still bothering him over the events of the last day or so, but he had to admit that he would really like to have something to eat, even if his stomach was still upset.

"I know how I can get myself food, and I am sure that I can bring some back for you, but I promise you that it's not going to be a five star four course meal or whatever," Anastasia said shaking her head.

"After getting used to eating nothing but soup and potatoes I guess I can't really complain about anything that you managed to find. But how do you intend to find food in the middle of the forest like that?"

"Well I'm not going to find the food; my wolf is going to find the food."

"But I thought you said that when your wolf ended up eating something that it usually gave you indigestion."

"Over time my wolf has gotten a little bit used to eating whatever she can find, and under the circumstances I think that anything is better than nothing. At some point we're going to have to find food, and the sooner we find food the better off we will be. So I think that right now I should go out and hunt, as the Germans won't be looking for a wolf, you can stay here and guard the cave and I will bring us back something to eat."

Ivan had to admit that he began blushing as Anastasia started sliding out of her clothing and arching down on the floor. He decided to be a gentleman and look away, which she said was rather sweet of him, although under the circumstances she didn't really feel all that bashful, as he had already seen everything, so she really had nothing to hide. Once you've seen someone naked you've seen them and can see them forever in your memory.

But he had to admit that there was something about seeing her transform into a wolf, while a thing of beauty, was also still rather startling, no matter how many times he witnessed it. Luckily the transformation to become a wolf looked less painful than the transformation back. It didn't take her long until she had transformed fully into her animal form, let out a small howl and started scampering off outside of the cave, leaving her clothing in a pile at the mouth of the cave.

As Ivan sat there near the mouth of the cave holding his pistol in case any Germans came, he found himself once again contemplating the strangeness of the situation he suddenly found himself in. It seemed like practically overnight he went from living a normal ordinary life of a teenage farm boy, to now playing survivor in a cave with a girl who turned into a wolf, all as though it were nothing unusual.

Then he thought to himself was it really all that unusual? Now that he had accepted the existence of werewolves he had already seen her transform several times, and it was already becoming routine, as crazy as that sounded. He figured he should be thankful that he had someone as wonderful as Anastasia who actually trusted him that much.

However he couldn't help but be thinking of all his family and friends back in the village. Surely Anastasia must be as broken up about the loss of her family as he was about his, but he had to admit that she seemed like the stronger person, which made him feel that he was unworthy of her, but then how do you live up to the expectations of a girl who can turn into a wolf? She was certainly no ordinary woman, and he was feeling very much a very ordinary boy, albeit one in rather extraordinary circumstances, even if supposedly by virtue of his bar mitzvah he could consider himself a man.

Then he started thinking about everything they had talked about, and he started feeling better about his situation. She did in fact find him worthy; in fact she seemed to think that he was a cut above the ordinary, seeing as she was right that the average person, having seen what he had seen, probably would have run for their lives. In fact now that he thought about it he wondered why he didn't run for his life when he first saw her transform, as that would have been a perfectly normal reasonable response, under the circumstances.

Maybe it was just because she was in a position of vulnerability, maybe he was just in a state of shock over what he was witnessing, but maybe it was because deep down he knew that even if that girl was a vicious animal it was still the Anastasia that he knew and had loved from afar for so long, and now that he was loving up close.

As he waited for Anastasia to return, all of these thoughts continued to occupy his head, and he found himself getting a headache. It was probably from the lack of food and water, so he was hoping that she would be back soon with something to eat. The longer she was gone the more he began to worry however, what if she did encounter the Germans, what if they shot her just for the sport of it?

He didn't want to contemplate that possibility, Anastasia was the only thing he had left in the world, and if he lost her that would pretty much be it for him, he would have nothing left to live for and would lose the will to go on. But as long as she was alive he figured that there was still hope for the future, although what kind of future he was going to have with her in this new world they found themselves in was anybody's guess.

Eventually Anastasia returned with what looked like a small animal in her mouth that she came into the cave with and dropped on the floor at his feet, almost like some type of cat who had brought a mouse back home. He remembered one time when the family cat had brought a mouse home, completely mutilated, and Igor began playing with it as though it was alive.

He found himself silently laughing to himself before he began to get watery in the eyes again as he thought of his poor dead brother, his poor dead brother who would never again kill another mouse and have fun with it. As he looked at the little remains of the critter on the floor in front of him, he thought it was rather funny that Anastasia's wolf was behaving like a common house cat.

Once she had dropped the animal on the floor however, her wolf started slowly walking over to where her clothing was and stretching out, and starting to make those violent and excruciating noises, as her body violently snapped back into place like a rubber band.

That was something that he preferred not to watch, he had to admit there was something that made him squeamish about seeing her body contort in so many ways that shouldn't be possible for a human girl. That part was certainly nothing sexy, at least to him.

Once Anastasia had finished getting dressed she came over and shook her head. "I have to admit, that not having any hands, I was unable to gather any firewood."

Ivan smiled. "Gathering firewood is something that I am kind of an expert at." He handed her the pistol. "Here, you can use this to defend yourself while I am gone."

She pressed his hand with the pistol away and shook her head. "No, I think that you should hold onto it, what if you encounter soldiers out there again, it would be your only line of defense."

"But what are you going to do for protection?" Ivan suddenly started laughing as he remembered. "I'm sorry, I keep forgetting that you can take care of yourself."

"If anybody tries to come again me don't worry I can transform rather fast, even though I would rather not have to tear out of my clothing," Anastasia said with laughter, as once again Ivan found himself blushing at the thought of her ripping out of her clothing in wolf form. One thing that he hadn't even thought about up until then that every time she was in her wolf form she was, technically speaking, completely naked, even if not a naked human and who was well covered by fur. Maybe he still was thinking like a typical teenage boy in love, albeit with a far from typical teenage girl.

"I won't be long," Ivan said, and he truly did intend to be as quick as possible, as he didn't know what was out there and he was eager to get back to Anastasia. "I wish that I had something we can gather water in."

"Well I know that there is a stream back in the cave, so don't worry, we will have a source of water when we need it," she said as she pointed to the back of the cave. "Like I said I know this cave like the back of my own hand, or paw, as the case may be."

Ivan laughed again before nodding and slowly emerging from the cave. Fortunately he didn't see any sign of the Germans, or hear any signs of explosion or gunshots. Maybe they had already stopped looking for survivors, although he didn't think that that would be the case for very long. He quickly went into the woods and gathered up as much firewood as he could as quickly as he could. He had to admit that he felt lonely doing so without his brother, as much as he complained about his brother always tagging along and being a nuisance and not very much help, he had to admit right now he would give anything to hear Igor's voice saying how he found a mouse right before he snapped its neck and started laughing and smiling his big stupid smile over it.

Ivan got back to the cave with enough firewood to at least start one fire at any rate. Fortunately he knew how to make a fire by rubbing sticks together, so they weren't going to starve at any rate.

"I guess we will have to just eat it with little bits of fur in it, seeing as we have nothing to clean it off with, which I think I am a little bit more used to then you are perhaps," Anastasia said.

"Right now I'm so hungry I'm not even going to be very picky about it," Ivan said as they began cooking what Anastasia had brought into the cave over the fire that they had started. Ivan had to admit as he started eating this small little animal, it didn't taste as bad as he thought, but at the same time it made him long for the days when he could rely on soup and potatoes every morning, however meager an amount.

For the most part they ate their meal in silence, and Anastasia didn't seem like she was the least bit squeamish about eating animals like that with her bare hands, and there were not many girls that he knew who could say that. She really was a step above the average woman, but once again that made him feel like much more of a very average boy by comparison, bar mitzvah be damned!

Once their stomachs were full Anastasia showed him where he could find the underground stream so that he could drink his fill. Then the two of them continued to sit in front of the fire that they used to heat their food and reflected on the fact that at least it made the cave a little bit less cold and a bit more inviting, but hopefully not to the Germans.

As the two of them sat there carefully guarding the mouth of the cave for any possible intruders, he felt Anastasia's hand on top of his and she was squeezing it tightly, as he realized that for the first time since any of this began she was silently sobbing and resting her head on his shoulder.

He simply sat there and let her, and in a strange way, in spite of everything that happened, something about the moment was just perfect, and he had never felt closer to another human being, werewolf or otherwise, and for the first time truly in his life he no longer felt completely alone.

It was their first day.

9

Over the next couple of days, Ivan and Anastasia eventually got into a fairly steady routine of spending most of their days together in the cave, often waiting until cover of night to go look for something to eat. Sometimes they didn't bother leaving the cave at all, as they could sometimes find fish in the underground streams and they were able to eat those, which they found might have been the path of least resistance, seeing as they had food right there inside of the cave with them, and fish were easier to cook and to clean than a lot of other animals out there.

"You really don't think that I am a monster Ivan," Anastasia said as they cooked their fish over the fire that night.

Ivan looked her directly in the eyes, her face flickering and forming shadows on the wall illuminated by the fire in front of them. "I could never possibly in a million years think of you as a monster. Even when I first saw you turn into a wolf I didn't really think that you were a monster."

"Really?"

"Okay I'll admit, when I first was wondering about you becoming a wolf like that I was kind of wondering if you were going to eat me, but deep in my heart I never seriously thought that you would. Do you really think that I would have gone to the summer festival you with you if I really thought you were going to kill me?"

She smiled. "I guess that's an interesting way of putting it, I suppose I probably wouldn't go to a festival with a person I thought was going to eat me, but then it depends how attractive they were I suppose."

Ivan began blushing as Anastasia started laughing. It was good to see her laughing, because after everything that had happened there hadn't been that much to laugh about lately, so every moment of lightheartedness that broke the tension was a welcome change of pace from the grimness of their surroundings.

"Don't worry Ivan, I wouldn't eat somebody that I found cute, so you are in the clear," Anastasia said as he continued blushing and she continued laughing hysterically. "Sorry I'm probably making you really uncomfortable and everything like that."

Ivan had to admit he had never spent so much time in close quarters with a woman who wasn't a blood relative like that, certainly not an attractive girl his own age like Anastasia, so this was sort of new territory for him, along with everything else that was new about this.

"Hey if it doesn't make me uncomfortable the fact that you turn into a wolf, then I suppose nothing else should make me feel uncomfortable either," Ivan said. "I guess I'm just sort of a little bit shy around, you know girls and stuff."

Anastasia smiled. "So you are more afraid of and intimidated by the fact that I am an attractive teenage girl than the fact that I am a werewolf, well that really says something!"

The two of them laughed, and for a moment it seemed like they were about to kiss, when all of a sudden Anastasia hesitated.

"Is something the matter?" Ivan asked, thinking that he had made another faux pas.

"Nothing, I was just thinking that maybe you really are afraid that I'm going to eat you," Anastasia said. "I mean food is getting kind of scarce around here and I can't make any promises."

The two of them continued laughing, and it was good that they were breaking the tension of the situation. Ivan could see that Anastasia was doing her best to try and make him feel comfortable with the situation, and he thought that it was crazy that he had to admit he was more shy about the fact that she was a girl than the fact that she was a werewolf, she was entirely right about that, and here she was trying her best to make him feel comfortable, when really he should be the one trying to make her feel comfortable.

"Anastasia can I ask you a question?"

"What is it Ivan?"

"Does it hurt?"

"Does what hurt?"

"When you become the wolf, or when you transform back, it's just, I mean I wasn't staring or anything, it's just, well it looks really painful."

"It's kind of difficult to explain. The wolf is part of me just like I am part of the wolf. It's like when I can feel her taking over I usually have some type of warning, so luckily she gives me time to undress and assume the position, I guess you would say. It's hard to say how I know that she wants to come out, it is just sort of a feeling in your gut, sort of an urge to give in, give into sort of a primal instinct. Then when I am her I feel both myself, but at the same time I feel her instincts taking over. I never fully lose control, and I always do come back, but it's like I am two different people at the same time, myself and the wolf."

"But does it hurt?"

"Transforming into the wolf doesn't hurt all that much, it's more gentle, but when I want to come back, particularly if I want to come back quickly, it feels like your whole body snapping back into place, it's sort of like a jolt, and it can be rather unpleasant. But after all of the other painful things we have seen in the last few days turning into a wolf and turning back from a wolf, well let's just say it's not the most painful thing in the world."

"You are really brave Anastasia, you know that."

"You are brave as well Ivan; don't let anybody tell you otherwise."

Ivan shook his head. "No, it's not the same way; you are brave because you are dealing with something out of the range of normal human experience. I don't know how I would react if I suddenly found myself spontaneously turning into a wolf like that, I mean I don't even know how you process something like that."

She shrugged her shoulders. "I guess I just never really gave it much thought, it just became a part of my life, and I guess when it's part of your life like that you just get used to it, it just seems normal. I know that sounds really strange, how can turning into a wolf like that ever seem normal, but after it has happened a few times you just sort of get used to the fact that it's going to keep happening, and as far as I know it will keep happening for the rest of my life. But sometimes it does make me feel like a freak, or even a monster."

"You are not a monster; the real monsters are the people who are out there that we are hiding from. In a world where people like that go around slaughtering innocent people indiscriminately for no particular reason, and you haven't hurt anything bigger than a small animal, don't let anyone ever try to tell you that you are a monster. You are a majestic creature, like a force of nature."

Anastasia smiled. "You know I actually don't mind being out here in nature. Don't get me wrong, I miss my family and I miss my home and everything, but somehow this cave almost feels like a second home to me. Maybe it's the wolf talking, but it feels like I have always been living two lives, one life in society and civilization among normal everyday people, and this other part of myself that I always had to hide out here in nature, which sometimes feels more like my true self than my human side, more natural. Well it's just it's very refreshing that I don't have to hide this from you Ivan. You are the first person who has accepted me for what I am."

"Have you ever told anybody else?"

"Well come to think of it, no I haven't, I have always kept it something of a secret, even from all of my closest friends and family. It's not exactly something you go around telling everyone, know what I mean?"

"Yeah I see your point about that, if I found myself turning into a wolf I honestly don't know what I would tell other people, I would be worried that people would think I was crazy."

"I suspect my grandmother knew, I don't know how she knew, maybe because she was able to read my palm, but she always knew that there was something different about me."

"Maybe she was a werewolf as well; maybe it's something that is passed down from generation to generation."

"Maybe, but if she was she never told me about it. The honest truth is I have no idea where this came from, and so far I haven't met another person like me, or rather another werewolf. I have never met another of my kind, for all I know I might be the last or only one in the world."

"But what about all of those legends of werewolves from the Middle Ages and other times and places like that, you certainly couldn't be the only one, those myths must have a basis in fact. Even our professor seemed to suggest that myths didn't come out of thin air, even though I don't think that he would ever allow himself to admit to the existence of werewolves, even if he had seen what I had seen."

Anastasia laughed. "I actually would have loved to see the look on his face as he saw me turn into a wolf, although not so much the look of him catching me undressing in the middle of the forest, that would be creepy."

The two of them laughed nervously as Anastasia knew that Ivan was still a little bit uncomfortable about those intimate matters like that.

"At any rate, I don't think that I am ever going to meet another of my kind, and if I am the last in the world then I guess that just makes me even more special, doesn't it," Anastasia said.

"The way I see it you are special whether or not you are a werewolf, the fact that you are is just one more thing that makes you more interesting. I don't think that I would mind being a werewolf, I mean it looks painful transforming and everything, but it is still kind of awesome that you can actually do something like that, you are almost like superhuman or something like that."

"But I don't see myself as being superhuman, although sometimes I wonder whether this is a blessing or a curse, like with most things in life I guess it's a mixed blessing, if anything. I mean I don't dislike the wolf, sometimes I wish that she couldn't take over like that, but she is just as important part of me as this part of me and I wouldn't trade her for anything. Besides she saved both of our asses on more than one occasion."

"Well I guess that's something to be thankful for," Ivan said as they continued smiling. "Although I wonder how we are going to survive in the long term. I mean being in this cave with you is great and everything and I enjoy the company, but do you really think that we can stay here forever? I think at some point the Germans are probably going to come looking for us, and at some point we're going to have to have a life outside of this cave."

"You know sometimes when I am the wolf I can smell them coming, but I don't really smell them around this area at the moment."

"I just wish I had my knife so that maybe we could, you know, clean these animals and fish before we eat them, as well as have something additional to defend ourselves with."

He was wondering if she was thinking what he was thinking, but he didn't have to wonder very long because once again it seemed like she might have been a mind reader as well.

"You want to go back to the village don't you, see if there is anything left," she said.

"I'm kind of afraid of what we are going to find, but I think that we owe it to ourselves to, well I feel like we need a sense of closure, we need to find out if there were any survivors or if they left us any type of message. But it is probably not safe."

Anastasia shook her head. "You know if I went in wolf form I could probably smell them coming and warn us. Maybe we could go tomorrow and just scout it very quickly, just see what we can get in terms of supplies and –"

Ivan wanted to say that he wanted to see if there were any personal possessions that they could get, but he didn't want to seem like he was even thinking of materialism under the circumstances, although he knew that she fully understood as she probably felt similar.

"We will go tomorrow then, as long as the coast seems to be clear," Anastasia said as they nodded, finished their dinner and huddled up together for warmth as they sat around the fire and slowly went to sleep in each other's arms.

10

It was a warm summer night, and they both slept surprisingly well, and they woke up feeling unusually well rested the next morning. The sun was just poking in through the entrance of the cave, and they decided that they were going to go through with it, their plan from the night before.

"I think it's best that I go in the form of the wolf, you know so that my enhanced senses can allow me to smell or hear if there is any trouble coming," Anastasia said.

Ivan nodded as Anastasia stripped out of her clothing and once again began crouching down on the ground. Once again Ivan was a gentleman and didn't watch, but he still couldn't help but think of the fact that he was in a cave just inches away from a naked girl like that. Maybe he really was a very typical guy, thinking with a very typical mindset, even under the extraordinary nature of their circumstances.

But if she wasn't bashful he figured that it was kind of weird that he was.

Once Anastasia had fully transformed, Ivan put the pistol at his side and prepared to head out. Anastasia took the lead, as she could smell her way through the forest better than Ivan could, and having gone to the cave numerous times from the village she knew the best way to find her way back.

As they were walking along the path back to the village, Ivan began to feel a sense of foreboding as he looked at dead bodies strewn on the ground, all of whom were decomposing. This was telling him that maybe they should turn back.

"It must be terrible that you can probably smell those bodies better than I can," Ivan said patting Anastasia on the head. She looked up at him with sad eyes but she continued walking in the direction of the village.

Once again Ivan thought to himself it was extraordinary what anyone could get used to. The fact that they could just so casually stroll by lots of dead bodies strewn along the ground without paying them any care would have seemed unimaginable just a few days before, but if you stopped to be sick at the horror around you then you would be consumed by it, it could very well cost you your life.

After a time they finally he came to the borders of the village, and they both stopped short in their paths as they saw it. There was literally nothing left, the entire village had been wiped off the face of the earth. There were dead bodies strewn all about, most of whom that had been decomposing to the point where you couldn't tell who was whom, and maybe that was for the best, Ivan didn't really want to know if his friends and relatives were the bodies that were lying around strewn about what remained of the village.

"I guess we should be quick," Ivan said as he went to where his home used to be, but where now there was just a pile of ashes. His house had never been much of a palace, but it always been adequate for him, and now there were nothing left but memories. The chicken coop, the barn, everything that he and his family had had in the world was just completely wiped out by a bunch of ruthless invaders, who most likely pillaged everything, and then what they couldn't carry they set on fire.

Although he knew Anastasia would alert him to any trouble, Ivan took no chances, and he always had his hand right at his side ready to pull out the pistol at a moment's notice. Of course if he encountered an entire army of soldiers he was as good as dead. One clip of ammo wouldn't get him very far, at the absolute most maybe he would get a few lucky shots in and manage to steal a better weapon from whoever he managed to kill, and again that was if he was lucky, as he was no trained soldier.

In fact as he thought back to the other day, when he had shot those Germans, he thought to himself that that was the only time he had ever used a weapon, and even now the thought of doing so again was making him feel sick to his stomach, that combined with the smell of death in the air that could not be avoided. Everywhere he went there were swarms of flies making fast work of the dead bodies the invaders had left in their wake.

Ivan found himself feeling even sicker as he came to where his house had been and where his room had been. However, through some miracle, that was when he saw it, out of the corner of his eye, shimmering in the sunlight, it was his knife, a knife that his grandfather had given him, almost like a family heirloom.

He reached down into the charred remains of his home and picked up the one thing that had survived, strangely enough the one thing that he was actually looking for. As he held up the knife and looked at it in the sunlight shining brightly he had to admit that he felt the urge to plunge it into a German soldier's throat. The thought of shooting one a moment ago had made him sick, but now something about what he had witnessed around him, the sight of so many dead bodies, the bodies of all of his friends and family from the village, that was making his blood boil, now he wasn't just sick, he was sick and desiring of revenge.

However he composed himself and looked for a couple of containment vessels that they could use to drink water from. Only a couple of them managed to survive, a couple of them that were made of metal, metal was pretty much the only thing in the village that wasn't completely burned away to nothingness.

Ivan walked over a few paces down to where Anastasia's home had been, where he saw her wolf letting out a low howling noise, a mourning noise, a way of saying goodbye to everybody in the village. He stood there next to her and they observed a moment of silence. Ivan instinctively found himself folding his hands in prayer, even though he had never been a particularly religious individual. If there was a God he had a lot to answer for, and at that moment, aside from Anastasia, Ivan felt that he was quite alone as far as the supernatural forces of the universe went.

"I guess there is nothing more for us to see here, let's go to our new home," Ivan said as they began walking into the forest. They continued walking, Ivan not saying anything, seeing as Anastasia couldn't exactly respond aside from a bunch of growls and howls and moaning noises, which made trying to have a conversation rather difficult.

As they continued walking in the forest, Ivan did his best to ignore the dead bodies around him, and the smell of death everywhere he went. Even the birds didn't seem to be chirping, as though they were observing a moment of silence for the mass slaughter, for the massacre that they had witnessed. He kind of wondered what birds thought when they saw human beings behaving in such a disgusting manner towards one another, whether they understood the full inhumanity of the moment, even when they were not themselves human, but then being a wolf didn't take away Anastasia's humanity, didn't make her any less human.

Suddenly Anastasia stopped walking and started growling off in the distance. She then took off and started running towards the bushes, and that was how Ivan knew that he should do likewise. Soon they were crouching down in the bushes, once again hiding for their lives and trying not to breathe very heavily.

Looking through the leaves of the bushes, Ivan tried to get his best view of what was going on, and as soon as he had done so he wished that he hadn't. He wanted to close his eyes, but he knew that this was something that he couldn't close his eyes to, it was something that he had to bear witness to, as painful as it was.

He saw a long line of German soldiers marching a bunch of naked men and women in a line until they were all lined up in the dirt. They started taking shovels and they began digging what looked like a trench. Ivan thought that they should try to get out of there, but now it was too risky, as somebody could see them.

Ivan once again continued crouching down with Anastasia just a few inches away as they both looked on in horror, as it appeared that the German soldiers were now making these men and women, these innocent men and women, look like they were digging their own graves.

For a moment he wanted to shout at them that they should run, but then he remembered that they weren't running for the very same reason that he wasn't, because there was nothing they could do. If they tried to run they would be shot, although the way he saw things they didn't have all that much to lose anyway, as it looked like they were going to be shot one way or another.

The German started shouting something as the men and women began kneeling down. The Germans raised their guns and slowly and carefully went up and down the rows machine gunning the people into the trenches, their dead bodies falling into the pits, which must have been rapidly filling up with blood.

Ivan could feel himself choking vomit into his throat again and trying his best not to be sick, but there was little he could do other than to throw up as quietly as possible to the side. Here he was witnessing a scene of mass murder and there was absolutely nothing he could do about it. He clutched the pistol tightly, ready to spring it at a moment's notice, but he knew that if the enemy found him now that he would be just as dead as all of the people who had just been machine-gunned into their own graves that they had freshly dug. They were basically sitting ducks.

"See, these are the true monsters," Ivan whispered to Anastasia, knowing that with her enhanced hearing she would be able to hear it, even though he barely muttered it.

As line after line of people came over and were shot and fell into the trench, Ivan could hardly contain his rage. The sheer helplessness of having to watch something like that and not being able to do anything to stop it made him feel like a coward, but he realized that his instinct towards self-preservation wouldn't allow him to get himself killed for no reason, especially when Anastasia was there. He was more concerned for her than he was for himself, not that she couldn't take care of herself, but because he needed her more than she needed him, and he couldn't picture life without her, nor could pretty picture himself getting killed and leaving her alone in the world.

Ivan could feel the pistol trembling in his hand, as he was finding it hard to hold this hand steady. He knew that at any moment he might have to open fire, and even though moments before he had been fantasizing about revenge he knew that if he drew any attention to himself that he was as good as dead.

Anastasia started backing up, as Ivan could see that the soldiers were walking in their general direction. He didn't know what course of action to take, remain hidden and risk being found, or try to run and almost assuredly be shot in the escape attempt.

As nonreligious as he was, he found himself saying a silent prayer to God that if he was going to die right now to at least make it quick, at least let him die with some degree of dignity, and not as a coward in front of Anastasia.

As the German soldiers were only a couple of paces away, he considered taking the pistol and putting it into his mouth and firing, rather than risk being captured and dying a degrading death like the people he had just seen moments earlier, but he just didn't have it in him, he was a survivor, and if he was going to die he was going to die fighting, not die as a coward.

As the German soldiers approached, all the sudden a sound

of gunfire and explosions came out of nowhere and the soldiers started falling down. The German soldiers started fighting back and firing into the forest as Ivan took to the ground with Anastasia as they both laid on their bellies, trying to stay low to avoid getting hit with stray gunfire.

It was all going to be over soon, Ivan told himself, one way or another.

"I love you Anastasia," he said as his eyes began to water and he closed them tightly, expecting the blow of death, when all of the sudden he heard somebody move aside the bushes and turned around to find himself facing the barrel of a gun.

When he saw that his resolve failed him and he found himself dropping the pistol to the ground and preparing for the inevitable.

This was going to be how he died.

11

Ivan closed his eyes really tight, if he was going to be shot through the head he felt like he wanted his eyes to be closed, not that he felt that really made a difference, because if he was going to get shot through the head and killed one way or another it wasn't going to make that much of a difference how it happened, but he thought that it was just instinctive that if you are about to die that you would close your eyes so you wouldn't see it, at least that was the logic he was following in that moment where he thought that the end was approaching.

As a moment passed without anything happening, he gradually opened his eyes to see the man withdrawing the gun from his face and offering him his hand.

"Come with me my boy, I am not going to hurt you," the man said as he helped Ivan up and looked at Anastasia. "It seems this wolf is rather friendly with you."

"She's a little bit more than a wolf, I can't really explain right now," Ivan said, not exactly sure if he should be shouting that Anastasia is a werewolf to the entire world. Under the circumstances it may seem like he was just panicking and shouting all sorts of random crazy things, but he didn't want anyone to harm Anastasia.

The man nodded. "I understand my boy, when I was younger I knew a fellow in the village who was close to the wolves, even though everybody thought that they were dangerous. But just because an animal looks vicious doesn't mean that it's a killer, and you'd be surprised at how you can domesticate certain animals."

"She's no killer, but I don't think that she's going to be easily domesticated," Ivan said as Anastasia let out sort of a moaning howl and he began laughing.

"My name is Alexander and I am a member of the resistance, we will take you to safety," the man said as Ivan and Anastasia followed behind him. It seemed like there was an entire militia of people who were shooting at the Germans and firing into the dead bodies of the Germans to make sure that they had finished the job. Ivan tried to look away, as he would rather not witness any more death, even if in this case the people who were being shot were the people who were trying to kill him just moments before.

Alexander told Ivan to get down at points so that he could fire into the woods, as it seemed like the Germans were putting up a pretty fierce fight, and Ivan realized at that moment that he could be hit by a stray bullet at any second, although it didn't really occur to him the full implications of that. In the moment he was just intent on getting out of there and making sure that he got Anastasia to safety as well.

Alexander continued to lead Ivan and Anastasia through the forest, as the sound of gunshots and explosions off in the distance grew quieter and quieter until it was nearly silent. Finally they arrived at the outskirts of what looked like a makeshift camp full of tents. It looked pretty crude, but it looked like there were a fair number of people, and it looked like they had food and supplies and a place to stay.

"You're welcome to stay here, you are among friends here," Alexander said.

"It's a wolf!" a woman shouted as she came over making the sign of the cross, as though she had just seen a demon or a monster or something like that.

"Don't hurt her, she is friendly, I can't stay here without her," Ivan said as he kneeled down on the ground and hugged Anastasia with his arms and shielded her with his body.

"It's okay Svetlana, the wolf is not going to hurt anyone, it seems the boy has her well-trained," Alexander said, to which Anastasia let out another howl. "Or maybe she has him well-trained," he said with laughter as Anastasia began licking Ivan. "I've never seen a wolf behave in such a friendly manner before."

"Like I said, she's kind of more than an ordinary wolf," Ivan said, again not exactly wanting to explain at the moment that she was a werewolf, as he didn't want to be thought crazy among his new friends. "Do you think you can get her some clothes, unfortunately I left her clothes back in the cave, and I think that she would be a little bit bashful without some," Ivan said realizing that asking for clothes for a wolf probably wasn't making him sound any less insane.

"Your wolf wears clothing?" Svetlana said.

"I'm probably going to need to do some explaining, but yes, my wolf wears clothing, so can you please get her something to wear and maybe give her some privacy," Ivan said.

Svetlana sort of rolled her eyes at Alexander, who sort of nodded off into the distance as Svetlana went back to one of the tents and came out with a simple peasant's dress and handed it to Ivan.

"Come on Anastasia, I will give you some privacy," Ivan said as he led Anastasia into a tent and put the clothing down on the floor and zipped the tent up.

Ivan stood guard outside of the tent as Anastasia made loud noises of pain as she transformed back. He always hated the sound of her body contorting and snapping back after her transformation from a wolf, and as people outside of the tent looked off in the distance and could see her shadow go from the shadow of a wolf to the more feminine image of a woman, pretty much all eyes were on the tent.

"Is everything okay in there," Alexander said, as Ivan put his hand up, indicating that he should stay put and just wait for her to do her thing.

A moment later Anastasia came out of the tent wearing the peasant blouse and looking like she was still a little bit shaken up by her transformation, as was often the case.

"You are right my boy, she definitely seems to be more than an ordinary wolf," Alexander said, his eyes wide with shock.

"I think that I should probably be the one to explain," Anastasia said.

Svetlana looked at Anastasia with the same level of incredulity and shock that you would expect from anyone under the circumstances.

"She's not a monster," Ivan said to Svetlana, who seemed to be examining Anastasia as though she were some type of intellectual curiosity. "But it does seem like she is about the same size as you."

"Thank you for the clothing, I appreciate it," Anastasia said as she did a little bow and curtsy and smiled.

"Get these young people something to eat, I suspect that we will have an interesting story around the campfire tonight," Alexander said.

Ivan and Anastasia sat down on a log in the camp, and people brought them some bread and some coffee for them to eat and drink. It was good to have actual food again, actual food that they weren't eating from the forest and that didn't give them indigestion and diarrhea the way eating animals from the forest like that tended to do.

Once they had some food and drink inside of their bellies, they settled down and they started telling their story, with several people in the camp gasping, but also believing what they had seen with their own eyes, a girl going into a tent as a wolf and coming out as a human.

"She isn't cursed," Ivan said, as he could see Svetlana was still looking at Anastasia with a look of distrust.

Svetlana shook her head. "I had always heard legends like that, but I never really thought that I believed them, I thought that they were just folk mythology from the old villages and everything like that. Maybe when I was a girl I used to fear that the wolves would come out on the night of the full moon, but I don't think I ever really believed in werewolves until now."

"I didn't believe in werewolves either, for what it's worth," Anastasia said shaking her head. "I only started believing in them when I became one, and as I already explained I still don't know how it happened or why, and I suspect I probably never will, but I have accepted it as part of me. And as I explained the full moon has nothing to do with it, although on the night of the full moon the wolf usually does get rather antsy and wants to come out. But I can change at pretty much any time; sometimes it's my decision, sometimes not. But at any rate I promise that I will not hurt you, my wolf doesn't harm those that she considers to be friends."

Alexander smiled. "Well I have heard a lot of whoppers in

my day, but seeing is believing. At any rate, werewolf or not, you are welcome to stay here for as long as, well as long as this terrible situation persists. We don't really have much here, but you are welcome to it, and we want to provide a refuge for everybody who is fighting our same mutual enemy. The enemy of my enemy is my friend."

"The Germans burned our entire village down, they didn't leave anything except a bunch of ashes," Ivan said. "As long as they are in our land and invading our land I want to do everything that I can to fight back against them, and what's more I want revenge."

"You shouldn't live for revenge my child, they say if you live for revenge you have to dig two graves," Alexander said.

"We have a whole village of graves that we need to dig," Anastasia said. "Everybody that we know was slaughtered by them, they left nothing, they were a destructive force, like a force of nature, except nature isn't so systematically cruel and precise. So I'm with Ivan on this one."

"How did this all happen," Ivan finally asked.

Alexander sat down on the log next to them and shook his head. "It was a sneak attack, blitzkrieg warfare they call it, and they strike like lightning out of nowhere and destroy everything in their path. They are relentless killers and mass murderers. We have reports that they are going all around the country and systematically rounding up and murdering people, particularly Jews and Gypsies and other minority groups."

"You know I never thought about the fact that I was a Jew except at my bar mitzvah, I only started thinking about it now when they targeted us for extermination," Ivan said.

"I knew people didn't like Gypsies, but I never thought that we would be just systematically targeted for mass murder like this," Anastasia said.

Alexander nodded. "Isn't that how it always goes, sometimes we only realize who we are when people are trying to kill us, when we are at our weakest moments, that's when we need our faith the most."

"Well it's kind of hard to have faith in a loving God after what we just witnessed," Ivan said. "They rounded up innocent men and women, and they just stripped them naked and shot them inside of their own graves. They literally made them dig their own graves, what type of monster does that? What type of just and loving God stands by and allows that to happen?"

Alexander shook his head. "I don't know my child, but I do know that the only way we are going to stop it happening again is to fight back. Our forces are limited, and the enemy is at the advantage, but I believe in not going quietly into that good night. Even if the odds are against us and seem hopeless, I always prefer fighting to surrender."

Ivan and Anastasia took sips of their coffee and nodded in agreement.

"I agree with you, but I have to admit that I am no soldier, in fact until the other day I had never even handled a gun before, and I just got in some lucky shots at most," Ivan said. "And I have to admit that afterwards I got sick."

Alexander patted Ivan on the shoulder. "There is nothing to be ashamed about my boy; under the circumstances you are very brave and very resilient."

"I've never killed anybody before," Anastasia said before hesitating. "At least not as a human."

"Her wolf saved us on a couple of occasions," Ivan said.

Alexander smiled and laughed. "Well it sounds like you have been given a gift there young lady. I don't have any explanation for what you are any more than you do, but whatever it is it seems like it has saved your life on more than one occasion, and it sounds like you know how to handle yourself, human, animal or otherwise. But everyone will be trained here to fight, so that we will be prepared when the enemy attacks again, because we know that they will come again and we want to be ready for them. But you both must be tired after everything you have been through, now that you have food in your bellies tonight you should just rest and recuperate, and we can begin your training tomorrow. I suspect that you probably haven't had a good night's sleep in a long time, and you would be amazed at how much it can work wonders to restoring you to your normal equilibrium. Come, we will find you a tent to sleep in."

Alexander only had one tent left to spare, and he figured that they didn't have a problem with sharing a tent together, given that they had been sharing close quarters in a cave for all of that time.

As Ivan and Anastasia crawled into their tent together and into their sleeping bags, Ivan thought to himself that even though they had been spending time together in the cave, this was the first really intimate situation that they seemed to really truly be in.

Anastasia started getting undressed; seemingly unbothered by the fact that Ivan was in the tent with her.

"You don't have to look away," Anastasia said as Ivan stopped covering up his eyes and looked upon her, standing there naked in front of him, his eyes locked on her and completely mesmerized.

After that it all seemed to happen so fast. Ivan stood up and Anastasia slowly slipped off of his clothing, undressing him as he blushed slightly and tried to resist the urge to cover himself up. Although he had seen Anastasia in this state many times before, this was her first time seeing him, and it was a weird feeling. He had never been with a woman before, and until he had seen Anastasia he hadn't even seen a woman naked before.

Natural instincts however took over, and the next thing they knew Anastasia was on top of him and they were going at it like animals in the tent. Little was said during the act itself, and it seemed like it was finished almost as quickly as it started, although it felt like it also could have lasted forever, their two bodies locked and intertwined like that.

Afterwards they laid next to each other in the tent, not exactly sure what to say to one another. The act was so spontaneous that they didn't even really discuss it, but Ivan knew that it was the most wonderful moment of his life, and he felt that for Anastasia it might have been as well. It was one scene of beauty and human intimacy and connection in a world that had gone insane and descended into the worship of death. But for just one moment, between the two of them, there was a moment of life, of love, and even something as simple as friendship.

Ivan fell asleep shortly afterwards feeling Anastasia's body pressed up close to his until he was awoken by Anastasia standing up in the tent.

"Is something the matter?" Ivan said, wondering if he had done or said something wrong.

Anastasia simply shook her head and smiled. "No, nothing is the matter, I just think, well what we did, I think that it has made her want to come out."

"Her," Ivan said before realizing what she meant.

"The wolf," Anastasia said as she started getting down on all fours and quickly transforming as Ivan stood there once again in awe of the majestic nature of it, of the fact that he was seeing something beautiful, something supernatural, something beyond the human explanations, that made the world all the more mysterious and special.

Ivan quickly got dressed, opened up the tent and followed Anastasia's wolf out into the forest where she went to the edge of the camp and let out a couple of low moaning howling noises at the moon, which while not quite full, was nonetheless still bright enough to chase away the darkness of the night, and as far as Ivan was concerned it was the most beautiful sight that he had ever witnessed.

12

The next couple of days passed in a fairly steady routine. Fortunately they didn't encounter any more attacks from the Germans, although they knew that they were out there and that inevitably there would be another confrontation, but they both wanted to be ready.

Ivan and Anastasia both trained in the use of small arms, as well as knives and other weapons of war, and they found themselves learning surprisingly fast under the circumstances, perhaps out of necessity, perhaps to keep their minds off of the situation at hand.

They felt that they were narrowly focused on survival, but the fact that they were now with another group of people with a similar goal made them feel clearer and better protected. There was strength in numbers, and you couldn't exterminate everybody unless they just sat back and let you. The attack on their village had been a sneak attack that nobody had seen coming, but now they knew that the enemy was out there and was looking for them, so it was in their own best interest to be as well prepared for the inevitability of that as possible.

The one thing that bothered Ivan though is that, although they continued to share a tent together, the spontaneous lovemaking of their first night together did not repeat itself. This made Ivan worried that he had done something wrong, or that maybe Anastasia didn't like it as much as he did, even though she seemed to be enjoying herself.

Now that they were safe and had a place to sleep at night and a steady source of food, however meager the rations tended to be, and however monotonous the meals were, gave them a lot of time to sit back and think and reflect on everything that had happened, and Ivan found himself reflecting a lot.

Finally though, one night Ivan could take it no more, and he felt that he had to say something, because it would drive him crazy if he didn't.

"Anastasia did I say or do something wrong," Ivan said one night as they were in the tent together after an exhausting day of training.

Anastasia shook her head. "Why would you think that you did something wrong?"

"But it's just after the first night we haven't; well I mean we haven't exactly –"

"Oh, I see is that what is troubling you," Anastasia said shaking her head. "I want to put your mind at ease as it was nothing that you have done wrong. That was probably the greatest night of my life in all honesty Ivan, but it was a spontaneous expression, something of the moment, something beautiful. I think it was something about the survival instinct kicking in, the force of life fighting back against the forces of destruction. And it's not that I don't want to do it again, it is just under the circumstances we probably need to be more responsible. We are guests here in this particular camp of partisans, and life is just so uncertain now, I guess what I am saying is I don't want to find myself having to worry about bringing a child into this world that we find ourselves in, I mean if werewolves can even get pregnant."

"Why wouldn't they be able to?"

She shrugged her shoulders. "I have no reason to suspect that they couldn't, but I just don't know Ivan, that's the thing, so why take chances? I don't say that to disappoint you or anything like that, I'm just being practical about these things, you understand right?"

"I think so," Ivan said, although he had to admit to himself he wasn't quite sure if he did. All of this was so confusing to him, and he suspected it was probably as confusing to her as it was to him.

"But there is another issue, I think that particular act of intimacy, that passion; well I think it kind of brings her out, if you know what I mean."

"You mean that what we did triggered your wolf to come out?"

Anastasia nodded before blushing slightly. She hadn't blushed before, as she seemed like she wasn't the bashful type, so the fact that she was blushing now was actually making him wonder why.

"Hey, you're blushing," Ivan said.

"Am not!" Anastasia said as she pushed him playfully and smiled. "But it's true, I think the fact that we gave into those passions, well I think that passion, just like anger and other strong emotions, I think that that's might what be what triggers the wolf to come out. Like you know how women's cycles are said to be by some people to be affected by the moon, or that they follow that cycle of the moon, well I think that the wolf is something like that, she has her own cycles as well, her own time of the month so to speak, if that makes sense."

Ivan had to admit that that made more sense than everything else that she had been talking about tonight, so he simply nodded his head in agreement.

"Don't worry Ivan, someday we will work all of this out, and someday this conflict will be over and then we will have all the time in the world to, well to get to know each other better, I guess you would say," Anastasia said as she kissed him on the cheek, and for him that was enough for now, and the two of them fell into a relatively deep sleep.

The next morning after breakfast of the soup and potatoes, that Ivan had grown to become bored of but now appreciated simply for the fact that they were there and he could rely on it, he and Anastasia did their training like they did every morning, but they realized that they were starting to stink.

Ivan decided that maybe he would take a bath in one of the communal bathing vessels that Alexander was able to heat up for him. While he was sitting there relaxing and washing off, that was when Anastasia came over with a smile on her face, as Ivan sort of covered himself up as she slid out of her clothing and got into the vessel with him.

"I hope you don't mind, but being a wolf and running through the forest doesn't exactly cause you to smell very nice either," Anastasia said as they both sort of laughed.

The two of them sat there getting nice and warm and

comfortable, both just sort of enjoying the moment but not saying much. Ivan couldn't believe that now he was sitting there taking a warm bath in the middle of the forest with the girl of his dreams, who was trying to wash the scent of the wolf off of her, but once again it was one of those few treasured moments of life that made him realize that he did want to go on living, and in spite of all the tragedy that they had both experienced they could both enjoy the simple things in life, and both had a desire to go on living.

Slowly Ivan and Anastasia began leaning forward, and just as their lips were touching in a perfect moment of unadulterated bliss, that was when all of the sudden they both jumped up out of the vessel before immediately crouching back down so that nobody saw them, as the sound of explosions and gunshots started echoing off in the distance.

"Everybody to their stations, we are under attack," Alexander shouted as Ivan and Anastasia quickly jumped out of their bath and quickly got dressed, not even concerned if anybody was seeing them, as everyone was too busy scrambling in all directions gathering their weapons.

Soon they had their own weapons clutched tightly in their arms as enemy fire started ricocheting through the camp, knocking down several partisans before they could even get a couple of shots in.

Ivan and Anastasia crouched down with Alexander, as it seemed like the gunshots were coming from every single direction. Many people started running and tripping in the confusion, but they figured it was best to lay low. German soldiers began advancing on them, and Alexander started running in the opposite direction from them. Shortly after that an explosive shell went off not far away from where Ivan and Anastasia were, causing them both to dive out of the way in opposite directions.

The two of them began firing in the same direction from which they were being fired upon, and it sounded like they might have been hitting something, but they weren't quite sure, as they couldn't see in all the confusion. More explosions elsewhere in the camp were causing their ears to begin ringing, and neither of them could hear what the other was saying.

Once some of the dust cleared, that was when Ivan noticed something, Anastasia was holding her shoulder and chest area and it looked like she was bleeding profusely from a wound of some kind.

"Anastasia, you're hurt!" Ivan shouted as she slowly started lowering herself to the ground and he put her up against a tree to try and look at her wound.

"Ivan you have to get out of here and save yourself," Anastasia said, gagging up and choking up blood.

"Do you actually think that after everything I'm just going to leave you here like that," Ivan said. "Come on, I will carry you on my back if need be."

Ivan smiled at her until all of the sudden he felt something hit him from behind, and he spat up blood, before he fell forward right on top of Anastasia.

"Ivan!" Anastasia shouted as German soldiers started running off in the distance. Although she was injured she could feel something bubbling up inside of her, and that was when all of the sudden it happened, completely spontaneously and without warning, she transformed into the wolf, tearing straight out of her clothing and immediately standing on top of Ivan and growling off in the distance. She wasn't about to leave him there to be finished off by the Germans, even though she could tell that he had a bullet in his back.

"How about that, it's a fucking wolf," the German soldier said as he approached, preparing to shoot Anastasia with his pistol, when all of the sudden Ivan leapt up stabbing the soldier in the stomach, wrestling him to the ground and cutting his throat before dropping his knife to the side and falling down on the floor once again.

"Anastasia get out of here," he said as he started drooling blood all over as he began gagging and coughing. In just a few seconds it seemed as though Ivan had stopped moving and breathing altogether, as Anastasia's wolf began howling at the Germans who were slowly surrounding her.

Not expecting her to engage them, Anastasia jumped forward and began biting one of the soldiers, quickly tearing into his throat, before diving on the other soldier, biting him in the crotch and then forcing him to the ground where she began scratching his face. She continued leaping on top of them, scratching and biting him, until all of the sudden he pulled out a knife and stabbed it into Anastasia's gut, causing her to yowl out in pain as the soldier threw her off of him and knocked her to the ground right where Ivan was.

The soldiers quickly began running away from the scene, with some cursing at the wolf specifically, as Anastasia stood there still standing over Ivan's body, which was no longer moving. Anastasia licked Ivan's face, smeared with blood, looked up once more at the sky and let out a loud painful howling noise, mourning the death of her companion, before laying down on top of him, slowly lowering herself on top of his body and closing her eyes.

As her body ceased breathing suddenly it made one final painful contortion as the body snapped back into that of a naked girl covered in blood on top of Ivan's body, two innocent victims of a world gone mad, and who shared a brief moment of beauty in that world, but who had now departed it together.

Epilogue

Alexander went through the forest looking for the place where it had all happened so many years ago. He only knew them for a brief time, but he knew that this is where they lived their last days with him before dying. He was one of the few survivors, but he felt that he needed to pay tribute to the two bravest people that he had known in the entire course of the war, that is why he paid to have the statue commissioned, even though people said that it was in the middle of nowhere, but it wasn't nowhere, it was to commemorate the scene of a massacre.

"Daddy is this where it is," young Anastasia said as she pointed to a statue of a small boy holding a pistol in one hand with his hand at his knife at the other, and at his foot was the statue of a wolf with her head looking up towards the sky making a howling stance.

"Come here young Ivan, I want you to see the statue of your namesake and the namesake of your sister," Alexander said as his two children stood there looking at the statue. "This is where it all happened, in such a short time that it seemed almost like it didn't actually really happen, or that it happened to somebody else. But I bore witness to it, I bore witness to so many terrible things during the course of the war, but this was one of the few things of beauty that came out of that war. Although they didn't survive they will live on in the memory of all those who did, whose lives they touched and inspired, the story of the boy and his companion, the girl who howled at the moon."

Bonus Stories
The Wolf Man of Auschwitz

He came with the new arrivals, and like all the new arrivals he was lined up at rollcall. He was a seemingly ordinary man with nothing particularly distinguishing about him, other than the fact that he got off the train completely naked. Oh well, I thought to myself, that would save them the trouble of having to strip him naked later on.

He seemed as though he were highly eccentric in some way, and I couldn't help but wonder why he came into the camp not wearing any clothing. But he appeared to be muscular and in relatively good shape, and that is probably why they selected him for work detail rather than sending him immediately to the gas chamber like the vast majority of people.

Later on, after they had dressed him in the standard prisoner uniform, he was assigned to the same barracks that I was. He came over near me and I wanted to say something to him but I didn't know exactly what to say. I noticed that he was wearing a black triangle, the symbol for mental illness or antisocial behavior. This suggested that he was put into the concentration camp possibly because he was crazy. But apparently they didn't send him immediately to die, probably because he was a muscular and fit individual and they figured they could probably get some good work out of him.

When we had retired to our barracks for the evening on the third day I accidentally bumped into him when I was getting ready to go to bed.

"Sorry," I said to which he simply nodded. I wanted to say more, but it didn't seem like the occasion to start up a conversation. I was always shy and socially awkward and the situation of being in the place where we were didn't exactly make me more sociable. You can never know who to trust here, and as far as I knew this man was mentally ill in some way, although given that going against the regime was now considered a mental illness in some places it is perhaps possible he was the victim of unfair classification, a legitimate political dissident. But he could also be a criminal, there was really no way to know.

As we were lying down next to each other I heard him counting as though he were counting down a set number of days.

The next morning on our way to rollcall I wanted to ask him something but I didn't want to be caught talking or the Nazis might beat me, so I decided to hold my tongue until after the long rollcall where we stood out in the cold as the guards made sure all of us were there. This took several hours and the whole time all I could do was stare at this particular man and wonder what had gotten him incarcerated here.

After rollcall we ended up being assigned to the same work detail in the metal shop and I decided that now would be the proper time to introduce myself.

"My name is Hansel," I said to him.

He simply nodded without saying anything.

"What happens to be your name?" I finally asked in frustration, kind of worried about how specifically he would react to my abruptness.

"Fitzroy," he said before going back to his work.

I wanted to ask more but I decided that now wasn't the appropriate time, and he seemed to be a very shy and taciturn individual, not all that unlike myself.

Later at lunch when we were eating our soup and bread I decided to be really friendly because I was quite curious. I offered him a very small piece of bread, even though I was starving and we never got enough food for even ourselves.

"For me?" he said as he examined the bread before handing it back to me. "I can't take this, you need it yourself, you are far more malnourished than I."

That was indeed true. I had already been here for several months and you could see my bones and my skin hanging off of those bones. He was relatively robust and healthy by comparison, having just arrived and not been subjected to prolonged starvation yet.

As we sat there eating I eventually worked up the nerve to ask him. "What were you counting down to the other night?"

He stopped eating for a moment, paused and looked at me. "What do you mean?"

"Last night in the barracks you were counting down to something, like you were counting down a certain number of days. I was kind of wondering what you were counting down to. I hope that I am not being rude or asking anything intrusive, it was just that I heard you counting down and it got me curious, and I guess my curiosity has gotten the better of me, because I can't stop thinking about it."

Fitzroy smiled and laughed. "You are a funny one."

"How so? I just heard a man mysteriously counting to himself as he was going to sleep and I kind of wondered what it was about. Were you counting sheep to fall asleep?"

He licked his lips when I mentioned sheep. "I would rather not think about sheep, thinking about sheep makes me just want to eat one. I would even eat one raw, and I have before."

"You've eaten raw sheep?"

"Let's focus on the first question, you asked why I was counting down or what I was counting down to. If you really want to know I was counting down how many days left until the full moon."

"We just had a full moon recently, so I think that we have a good while to wait. But why are you so concerned with the full moon? Are you planning to break out of here or something by the light of the full moon?"

He nodded. "You are very perceptive. Yes, I am waiting for the full moon to escape, if I can last until then it should be easy enough."

I looked at him with astonishment. "You seem overly confident about that. I have to warn you that if you try to escape they will most likely kill you. Very few people successfully escape from here and if they do they usually make others pay for it with their lives. If someone does manage to escape they often execute several people in retribution."

"Well I would not be happy about that, but we have to look out for our own well-being, and I firmly intend not to die here."

"You have some type of plan of escape? Maybe I can help you and join you if you really have a good enough plan."

He shook his head. "Sorry, I work alone. You would probably just slow me down."

"I can hold my own if you let me in on your plan."

"I'm afraid that this is something I have to do solo, you would not have as much of a chance as I do."

"And why is that?"

He laughed again.

"What's so funny?" I demanded. "Do you think that I would

not make it just because I am weak and sickly?"

He shook his head. "No, you wouldn't make it because you aren't a werewolf."

"Because I'm not a werewolf?!" I shouted before lowering my voice so that the guards would not get suspicious.

"That's right, I am waiting for the full moon when I will then transform into my wolf form, and using my added agility and speed I will be able to tear down any guards that get in my way and escape from here. By the time the full moon is gone and I transform back into a human I should be far away from here and hopefully across the border into a nation where I can find some sanctuary until this dreaded war is over."

I didn't know quite how to respond but then everything started coming together. The black triangle, mental illness, him appearing naked. He probably ran around naked thinking that he was some type of werewolf, they declared him mentally ill and they shipped him here.

"Anyway," he continued. "You had better not denounce me to the Gestapo and tell them my plan, or I will deny it, and I will get revenge."

"As if they would even believe that!" I shouted before lowering my voice once again.

"I didn't expect you to believe me, I don't even know why I told you. Best to just forget about it. But come the full moon I have every intention of getting the hell out of this awful place and regaining my freedom. I can easily survive in the forest, even in human form, by hunting and fishing."

By then our lunch call was over and we had to get back to work. I didn't really say anything to Fitzroy after that. I mean what you even say to a man who tells you something outlandish like that? My skepticism was fully justified and I pretty much just dismissed him as mentally ill and delusional.

I couldn't exactly blame him for that. Everyone copes with terrible situations in different ways, and believing that he was a werewolf was his way of coping, and probably what got him incarcerated here to begin with, which is pretty sad to think about, but I suppose we all have to look out for ourselves and can't concern ourselves with the plots and plans of others, and especially not with the rantings and ravings of a clear lunatic.

I didn't think much about Fitzroy after that. We saw each other every day, and we occasionally made some small talk, but for the most part we said nothing to each other. Each night I could hear him counting to himself and I found myself looking up at the moon each night and estimating how many more days until the full moon as well. Although I did not believe his claims I was still curious to see what would ultimately happen on that day and whether he would actually make the attempt to escape.

One thing I will say about Fitzroy though is that he had amazing endurance. Most people were worn down by the brutality of the camp rather quickly, but Fitzroy seemed to maintain an optimistic attitude and he didn't seem to require as much food as other people. Of course I didn't think that meant anything at the time, he was just a vigorous and healthy individual so he was not wasting away as quickly as others, but I had to admit that it was rather mysterious in a way that I took notice of.

Finally after about two or three weeks I noticed that tonight would be the night of the full moon and I was insanely curious to see what Fitzroy would do.

"So tonight's the night then?" I asked him nonchalantly.

"What are you talking about?" he asked me, probably surprised to see me asking him questions after having said nothing for the last couple of weeks.

"Tonight's the night of the full moon, still planning to make your big escape?"

He nodded. "I see you haven't forgotten about that. But don't get any ideas, I intend to do this alone and I can't have you slowing me down, so you will have to make your own escape plans if you hope to get out of here."

"Well I will wish you good luck at any rate."

"I know that you do not believe me, but watch me tonight and you will become a believer."

Later that night I couldn't help but feel excitement in the pit of my stomach, my empty stomach that would keep me awake every night with its growling. I'll admit that I couldn't even fall asleep because I was eager to see what would happen to Fitzroy. I almost thought that I should probably try to talk him out of it, because I almost assuredly expected him to get himself killed trying to escape. And even if he somehow managed to escape, it would be likely that several of us would be killed in reprisals, possibly even me, and for a moment that gave me a feeling of anger, that I could die because of his delusions of being a werewolf and trying to escape.

As the moon began rising, I saw Fitzroy stir from the barracks. He stood up and suddenly began taking off his prisoner uniform and standing there naked in the barracks. I thought that he had really gone crazy and that he was probably a few minutes away from death.

But then I saw something that I will never forget as long as I live and that I'd still sometimes find hard to believe if not for the events that were to follow.

As Fitzroy stood there naked in the barracks, he got down on all fours. I would have to admit that it was almost comical at first to see a grown man walking around naked on the floor like some type of animal. But then just as the moon first began to make its appearance I saw Fitzroy's body begin to slowly convulse and contort itself in ways that I didn't think were humanly possible.

Then he started making animalistic growling noises as he stretched out in all directions, and it sounded like he was in a tremendous amount of pain. Several people seemed to be awakened by the sound of his growling. It was almost certain that the noise he was making would attract the guards, and then we would probably all be in a great deal of trouble. I couldn't allow this to continue.

I started slowly approaching Fitzroy just as he fell to the floor and it seemed like the muscles of his body were rippling in every direction. Then it happened so quickly that it almost seemed like a blur. But I saw his fingernails start to grow into claws, and his back arched as a tail came out from between his butt cheeks, and his whole body began breaking out rapidly in fur.

I went to go and grab his arm, but as I did so he took a swipe at me and I could feel his claws scratch me across the stomach. I fell down to the floor grabbing myself. As Fitzroy stood up over me I realized that he no longer looked human, he looked like a gigantic humanoid wolf, standing upright. I stared him directly in his glowing eyes, and for a moment I felt completely terrified, as though he was going to devour me. Drool was dripping from his sharp fangs and dripping onto me. He came up close, sniffed me and then bolted off.

I started hearing shouts from the guards and I couldn't help but try to peek around the side of the barracks to see what was going on, in spite of the fact that I was in a tremendous amount of pain from the injury that I had just received.

I heard cries from the guards of "Wolf, wolf, there's a wolf out here!" I heard gunshots and then I looked around the corner to see a wolf bolting off and leaping over the fence as the guards fired several bullets into him, but it did not seem to faze him. Within a short time he had managed to escape and was already running off into the distance far away from the camp.

"He made it," I said as I grabbed my stomach and limped back to the barracks before collapsing, feeling assured that I would probably never wake up.

But the next morning I did wake up, and not only did I wake up, but I felt more vigorous and alive than I ever had before. I checked my stomach and I found that the wound had already healed, there was no sign of it. For a moment I thought that I had simply hallucinated and imagined the entire thing.

"Where is Fitzroy?" I asked, but the people around me just shrugged their shoulders.

We were then called to roll call and there was no sign of Fitzroy. In reprisals they killed 10 people by firing point-blank into their skulls. I was not among them.

At any rate, Fitzroy had escaped.

As I stood there during the rest of rollcall I found that I was not as cold as I normally was. I felt warmer, as though my blood was warmer. That day I was able to complete my work without feeling nearly as exhausted, and I gobbled down my food rapidly. I didn't feel as hungry, although I had to admit I had unusual thoughts of wanting to eat animals raw and rip them apart with my own teeth. I had been really hungry the entire time I had been imprisoned here, but I had never even come close to having fantasies that gruesome before.

These continued at night as I would dream of myself running through the forest hunting down and killing small woodland animals, as well as larger animals, like sheep. Suddenly those comments that I made about counting sheep to Fitzroy were put into greater context. He probably had eaten raw sheep, and wherever he was now he was probably surviving in the forest hunting small animals.

As time went on I began counting down to the full moon. Was I going to become a werewolf as well? I hadn't even believed in such things until I had seen Fitzroy transform in front of me. From what I had remembered of werewolf mythology if you get scratched by a werewolf you become one yourself. I was still skeptical, even in spite of everything that I had seen, but I couldn't deny that I was feeling lots of strange sensations and feelings that I had never had before, to say nothing of the unusual dreams and cravings.

Finally the night of the full moon did arrive, and during that entire day I felt myself becoming overwhelmed with aggressive feelings. I almost felt like challenging the guards before I realized how foolhardy that would be. If I could just last a couple of more hours I might be able to escape just like Fitzroy had. Sure it was a long shot, but after what I had seen him do I couldn't be quite as skeptical as I was before.

Then just shortly before the full moon began to rise the guards came to our barracks making a lot of noise. "Everybody rise!" the head guard shouted as several other guards pointed their guns at us.

Then one of the other guards came over and made an announcement. "We have uncovered evidence that several people here have been stealing metal from the workshop and using it to create weapons. Now if the guilty parties will come forward with said weapons the rest of you will be spared."

No one came forward, but I could feel my heart rate and pulse rate gradually accelerating, far beyond from just the nervousness of the situation. I was actually feeling extreme aches and pains throughout my body.

"Very well," the first guard said as he pulled someone out of line and put a gun to their head. "If the guilty parties do not come forward I am going to shoot this man in the head."

Nobody came forward.

"Very well then," the guard said as he pulled back his gun and fired a bullet into the man's head, causing him to fall dead to the floor with blood gushing out of his head wound.

Several people gasped, and while I was horrified at what I had seen, the other sensations throughout my body were causing me such overwhelming pain I could barely even pay attention to what was going on.

"Will no one come forward?" the guard asked again.

No one came forward.

"Very well then, I guess we shall continue," the guard said as he shot the next man in line. "We're going to keep playing this little game until somebody confesses."

They weren't very far away from me. If nobody came forward soon in a few minutes I would be dead. I thought that even if the Nazis didn't shoot me I might very well be dead shortly because I could feel like my entire insides were tearing themselves apart.

Finally I could take it no longer and I fell to the floor as I could feel my bones moving around inside of me as though they were going to snap.

"What are you doing, get up off the floor!" the guard said as he trained his gun on me.

I could not comply as I felt my body was tearing itself apart.

"What the hell," the guard said as several of the other guards all gathered around me.

Just as I could feel a gun pointed right into the base of my back and another gun in the back of my head I tried closing my eyes, figuring that I was seconds away from death. Then I saw a burst of light and the next thing I knew I found myself on top of the guards tearing them limb from limb. It was ecstasy as I bit into them and could feel the first guard being disemboweled. I then dove on top of the other two guards and threw them against the floor. Other guards began shooting at me but I bolted, finding myself running at incredible speeds that I didn't think possible. I also noticed that my vision had changed and I could smell and hear things that I had never been able to smell and hear before.

I saw the fence in front of me. One of the guards raised his gun at me but I knocked him to the floor and managed to dive over the fence. As soon as I found myself on the other side I ran as fast as I could, much faster than humanly possible, as the sound of gunfire echoed in the background.

The rest of the night after that was a bit of a blur. I seem to have vague memories of running through the forest and ripping apart a deer. When I finally came to I found myself lying naked in the forest covered in animal blood and feeling a bit sick to my stomach, although perhaps not hungry for the first time since I could remember.

It took me a while to regain my composure, but after assessing my situation I realized that I was quite far from where I had been imprisoned. I had somehow managed to free myself, or rather the wolf had managed to free me from my imprisonment. I had escaped.

I managed to find my way to a farm where I told a farmer my story about how I had been imprisoned in a concentration camp. They could have easily denounced me, and I could have been sent right back there, but they seemed like a sympathetic and decent couple. I of course didn't tell them about the fact that I had turned into a wolf, but they gave me new clothing and they managed to hide me for the rest of the war, which mercifully ended shortly after.

Miraculously I managed to survive. Although I still had a hard time accepting what had happened to me, I took no chances. Every month during the full moon I would make sure to lock myself up so that I would not harm any innocent people. It was a major inconvenience, but it was a small price to pay for being alive.

And alive I was. Becoming a werewolf, if nothing else, makes you much more vigorous. I managed to quickly regain my original weight, and I recovered from the long months of malnutrition and deprivation much more quickly than many other people who had been victims of similar. As many people died of epidemic diseases in the aftermath of the war I found myself strangely immune.

I never did see Fitzroy again or find out what became of him, but I always like to think that he was out there somewhere and that I owed him my life. I don't know if it was just an accident when he scratched me or whether it was intentional, but in any case I doubt I would have survived if it had not been for Fitzroy.

So now, once a month, as I transformed into a beast, I would acknowledge that I owed my life to the beast that I had become. And as I sat there in my cage locked away I would howl at the moon and I would always hold out the vague hope that somewhere out there Fitzroy was howling back at me.

I Was a Werewolf in the Hitler Youth

Rudolph had been looking forward to this day for so long, but it was finally his graduation day. He had spent his entire childhood in the Hitler youth learning how he would best serve the Fuehrer's army as an adult. Now he was on the verge of puberty and this was the day he would graduate to the next level, the level that every young member of the Hitler youth aspires to.

"Rudolph it's your turn," the doctor said as he waved Rudolph into his office. "Please get undressed and be seated." The doctor started looking over Rudolph. "I can see that you are a model of physical fitness, I am sure that your parents and the Fuehrer must be extremely proud of people like you. You should take to the transformation quite easily. You know this is now standard for most boys at puberty."

Rudolph nodded. "I have really been looking forward to it. You know I have wanted to be a wolf ever since this miraculous discovery several years ago."

The doctor smiled. "Yes young child, it really has turned the tide of the war in our favor. When Hitler's greatest scientists in the entire Reich isolated the infection that caused lycanthropy it was the greatest discovery in the history of medicine and practically ensured that the thousand year Reich would fulfill its goal of dominating the world. It is indeed a good time to be alive, and soon you will be a werewolf soldier in Hitler's army."

"I can't wait!" Rudolph said barely able to contain his excitement.

The doctor continued examining him. "Well you are definitely healthy and physically fit, so you should take to the transformation especially well. I have to warn you though; this isn't the standard puberty transformation. When your parents told you that you would start growing hair in unusual places at puberty they probably never anticipated that one day you would become a werewolf."

"Does this mean I'm going to turn into a wolf every time the moon is full?"

The doctor nodded. "But not only that, you will be able to transform into a werewolf at will. Sure it will take you a while to learn how it works and to get the hang of it fully, but I have no doubt that a boy who is as physically fit and intelligent as you will probably excel as a werewolf. I do warn you however, that the first transformation will be especially jarring to you. I am sure that all young boys in the Hitler youth like yourself probably think that being a werewolf is the greatest thing in the world, but the transformation can be quite painful and disorienting if you have never experienced it before."

Rudolph stood up and pounded his chest defiantly. "Trust me doctor, I am totally ready to serve the Fuehrer in his werewolf army. I have been looking forward to this for I can't even remember how long."

"Okay, but it is standard to keep you in a cage at first until we can train you to control the transformation. You are going to find that your senses are instantaneously heightened beyond your wildest imagination. You will be assigned to a wolf pack with other fellow members of the Hitler youth. You will learn to work together and function as an effective killing machine. Nature has found that the wolf pack is perfectly designed for military combat. Once you have learned how to transform into a werewolf at will and coordinate with other members of your pack you will be an unstoppable fighting force that will have the allies running in fear."

Rudolph nodded. "I look forward to it. So when do we get started?"

"Get into the cage boy," the doctor said as he opened up a large cage.

As Rudolph stood there naked in the cage, the doctor came forward with a rather large and painful looking needle, but he wanted to show bravery, to show that he was a true Nazi patriot. The doctor injected the needle deep within his muscle, and while it hurt, he had to admit as soon as it was injected into him he felt like he had a burst of energy.

"Now it is time to close the cage," the doctor said as he closed and locked the cage behind Rudolph. "Now we watch the transformation happen."

At first nothing seemed all that unusual. Rudolph suddenly realized that he started smelling things that he had not noticed just a few seconds before. He could also hear sounds off in the distance that he never would have been able to hear if his life depended on it just minutes before. His vision sharpened and he could feel a tingling sensation all over his skin.

Then all the sudden he started feeling himself convulsing, as though his bones were changing position in his body. He noticed that he was rapidly growing hair and that his teeth were growing long and sharp.

"I feel strange," Rudolph said as he saw his fingernails extend into claws.

"Do not be afraid, this is just a standard part of the transformation," the doctor said as he wrote something down on his pad. "I'm afraid that this is the painful part."

Rudolph began howling in agony as he felt his whole body convulse to the point where he fell on the floor, and it felt like every bone in his body was realigning itself. He continued howling as he got down on all fours and began arching his back. He could feel his tailbone extending until it was a full-blown bushy tail. The transformation only took a couple of moments before he found himself on all fours as a full-blown wolf. He immediately began howling at the doctor.

"Excellent, the transformation is complete!" the doctor said as he circled around the cage making observations of Rudolph's new physical form. "I can see that you have transformed into a healthy young wolf. How do you feel young Rudolph?" The wolf simply howled in return. "Yes, that is one of the disadvantages of being a werewolf, you can't exactly talk, but soon you will learn to respond to certain cues. Once your training is complete you will be able to function as part of a pack, and you will be able to read each other's emotions simply by looking at each other. Now I reckon you are probably pretty hungry."

The doctor went over and got a dish full of some type of meat and slipped it through a hole in the cage. Rudolph immediately began chowing down on the meat and began drooling.

"Yes, eat, build up your strength!" the doctor said as he smiled and laughed. "Now embrace your destiny!"

Once Rudolph had finished eating he went to sleep and a couple of hours later he woke up in the cage naked and cold, but once again fully human.

"Good to see that you are finally back with us," the doctor said with a smile. "So how are you feeling young child?"

"I felt extremely powerful, but it was kind of weird. I don't remember things the same way I remember things about when I was human. Being a wolf seemed almost like some type of really intense dream."

The doctor nodded. "This is all very normal, as it seems like humans and wolves do not process memory in the same way. When you have reverted to an animal state like that you are practically all instinct. But you will find that when you are in combat it will serve you well. You will be able to survive in the harshest of environments, and you will be able to rip apart your enemy with your bare teeth and claws. You should get a good sleep tonight, because tomorrow you are going to be joined with fellow members of your Hitler youth, and you will be trained for combat in your wolf forms. I am sure that you will find it extremely interesting."

Rudolph did sleep good that night, and early the next morning they had a hearty breakfast full of all sorts of different exotic meats that all of the boys gobbled down, like they pretty much were animals already.

"I am Heinrich Schmidt," the Nazi officer in front of them said. "And I am the one who is going to be teaching you how to spontaneously transform into werewolves and how to control yourself while in that form. At first you will find retaining your humanity while in your wolf form is not fully as easy as you might suspect. Your animal instincts will take over, but your human thoughts and feelings will still be there underneath. We will begin with trying to get you all to run through the forest and return back here and then transform back."

Heinrich took the boys outside where he instructed them to strip naked, despite the fact that it was freezing out. The boys all stood there shivering and rubbing themselves with their hands to try and retain some warmth.

"No doubt right now you are feeling extremely cold," Heinrich said with an evil smile. "That is to be expected. This is where turning into a wolf spontaneously will be important, as if you do not find a way to transform you will surely end up freezing to death. Trust me, as soon as you are in your wolf form you won't even be bothered by the cold at all, as you will have a thick fur coat protecting you from the elements. Now I want all of you to get down on your fours and channel the wolf within you. Concentrate on transforming into your wolf form. It may take a little while at first, but you should get the hang of it pretty quickly."

Rudolph found himself shivering, and he could already see his breath every time that he breathed. He tried to concentrate as hard as he could on turning into a wolf, but the feeling of freezing cold was distracting him from concentrating fully on the task at hand.

"I'm going to die of cold!" one boy shouted, which strengthened Rudolph's resolve not to show weakness in front of the other boys.

"Just concentrate on becoming wolves," Heinrich said as he went up and down looking at the boys standing there naked and shivering. "The fact that you need to become them in order to save yourself from freezing to death is all the motivation you should need. As you find your bodies freezing it will trigger the transformation in order to save yourselves."

Rudolph concentrated hard, and he could feel something inside of him, something jerking his body around in all sorts of different directions. He was proud of the fact that he was the first one to notice that he was transforming. He fell to the floor, and at first the cold snow numbed his knees, but as he felt his fur growing all over his body the feelings of cold gradually began to dissipate. Soon he was fully transformed, and he felt himself more resilient in the cold climate than he had just a few minutes ago.

"Excellent Rudolph, you were the first to transform!" Heinrich said as he came over and patted the boy on the head, to which Rudolph simply growled. "The rest of you should follow his example. If you don't want to freeze to death you had better transform soon. You know that the Führer will not tolerate weak soldiers in his army."

Rudolph watched as gradually the other boys in his unit slowly transformed into wolves, just like him, until all of them were now in their wolf forms.

"Excellent, you all transformed within a reasonable amount of time," Heinrich said. "With increased practice you will lessen the time that it takes you to transform fully. By the time you are ready to go into combat you will be able to transform practically instantaneously in the heat of battle. But for now we are going to start small. I want each of you to go into the forest and bring me back a rabbit. Go, Schnell Schnell!"

Rudolph and the other boys started darting off through the snow. Rudolph didn't know exactly how to find a rabbit, but then he found out that he had new instincts in his wolf form that he didn't have when he was human. He sniffed the air and he could get the scent of something, he didn't know how he knew, but he knew it was the rabbit in question. He soon started darting off and took chase after the first rabbit that he saw. The rabbit was swift but quickly ran out of energy, at which point Rudolph caught the rabbit between his jaws and dragged him back and dropped him at Heinrich's feet.

"And you are the first one to bring back the rabbit as well!" Heinrich said smiling and rubbing his hands together. "Excellent work Rudolph. As a reward you may now devour the rabbit."

At first the idea of eating a raw rabbit didn't sound very appealing to Rudolph, but as he smelled the rabbit wafting in the air he quickly became extremely hungry, and soon started tearing the rabbit limb from limb, and its flesh tasted delicious against his new more sensitive tongue.

Shortly after that the other boys came back with rabbits in their mouths which they soon devoured as well.

"Excellent, you all made excellent time in bringing back the rabbits!" Heinrich said smiling. "But Rudolph, as the first one to do so, will now be the leader of your wolf pack. In all matters you are to defer to his superior skills. Once you have finished devouring your rabbits you may concentrate on transforming back into your human forms and then get dressed. This is a good first day, but we will begin the combat training starting tomorrow. Small steps will lead to bigger things over time."

Over the next few days the training continued. The boys all shared a barracks together and boasted about who was the best werewolf. Rudolph tried to be humble, but he knew that he was the leader of the pack, and he retained that attitude even when he was in his human form.

"I'm going to kill dozens of Allied soldiers," Max, Rudolph's friend said.

"Well I'm going to kill hundreds," said Kurt, another member of his pack.

"I'm going to kill thousands," Rudolph said, and he meant every word of it.

The three of them continued to argue among themselves and the other boys, and as they got more and more aggressive they felt something brewing within them. Soon they started growling at each other and wrestling with each other. They felt stronger than they had just shortly before, being able to pin each other to the ground, and making loud howling noises as they did so.

"Rudolph, your hand!" Kurt said as he pointed to Rudolph's hand, which he now realized was turning into a claw. "You're turning into a wolf!"

"What is all the noise in here?" Heinrich said as he opened the door. "You are supposed to be sleeping, as you have a busy day ahead of you tomorrow." That was when he noticed that Rudolph's hand had become a furry claw which he quickly put behind his back. Heinrich simply smiled and laughed. "I see that you have gotten yourself into a hairy situation. This is nothing to worry about. When you get aggressive like that you might spontaneously transform into a wolf. What you will have to learn is that when that happens you can just as easily turn back by calming yourself down and focusing."

"You're not mad then?" Rudolph asked as he took his hand out from behind his back and looked at the sharp claws that were growing out of it.

Heinrich shook his head. "No, in fact I am impressed with you, spontaneous transformation like that is another good sign. Now see if you can focus on turning back."

Rudolph looked at his hand, or his paw rather, and he could tell that everyone was watching him and judging his performance. He started to slow his breathing and focus on being human again, and when he opened his eyes and looked at his hand it was once again fully human.

Heinrich patted him on the back. "Very good my boy, I can see that I did the right thing by making you leader of the pack. Now all go to sleep, like I said, you have a busy day in front of you, many busy days of serving the Führer."

The boys soon fell asleep, but Rudolph noticed that he was having all sorts of unusual dreams that night. He felt himself running through the forest chasing small animals and ripping them apart, and was thoroughly enjoying every minute of it. When he woke up he realized that he was sprouting an erection, which he found to be embarrassing, so he stayed under the covers until Heinrich came in and gave the wake-up call.

"Everybody stand at attention!" Heinrich said as he opened the door. When he noticed Rudolph's predicament he began laughing. "Nothing to be embarrassed about my boy, becoming a wolf often jump starts the libido and accelerates the process of going through puberty. Celebrate it, don't fear it. Embrace your wolf sexuality."

Rudolph had to admit it was an extremely embarrassing moment, but he did feel unusually powerful, so he simply smiled and nodded as Heinrich continued laughing and left the room.

When they went to go for breakfast they realized that there was nothing on their plates.

Rudolph raised his hand and Heinrich pointed to him. "Sir are we going to be given breakfast soon?"

Heinrich shook his head. "Part of your training is that you should catch your own food out in the wilderness. You will catch your breakfast and devour it while in wolf form. This will make you more effective soldiers if you can live off the land like that. So if you want to eat you had better transform very quickly."

All of the boys got undressed and got down on all fours and quickly transformed into wolves. This time the transformation was much more rapid, and Rudolph found that he didn't even need to concentrate all that much to transform into a wolf. Maybe it was because his stomach was so hungry, but he found as soon as he took on wolf form he was already hunting, and soon he had eaten three whole rabbits.

When Rudolph and the other members of his pack had finished their breakfast they all assembled around Heinrich who looked them all over. "Did we all eat well boys?" he asked laughing. "Very good, but today we have a special treat for you. Today you are going to hunt not rabbits and other small animals, but you are going to hunt full-blooded human beings. We have decided to give you something easy to start with, a couple of Russian POWs. They are malnourished and overworked, so they will probably be sluggish and easy for you to pick off. Consider this training for having to actively fight an opponent who actually has a chance. But for now we will start you off by acquainting you with killing human beings in wolf form. Use your noses to sniff out the prey. Now go, go and seek out the enemy!"

Rudolph took charge and the rest of his pack followed soon afterwards. He got the scent of the person in question. After running for a short while he saw a disheveled looking man dressed in little more than rags leaving a trail of blood from his frostbitten feet behind him.

Rudolph let out a loud howl signaling other members of his pack to begin circling around the man who picked up a stick and began waving it at them and shouting something in Russian that they didn't understand.

It didn't take long for all the members of the pack to begin attacking the man, and as Rudolph bit into the man's throat and delivered the kill he felt an immense feeling of pride like he had never experienced before. Not only was he the leader of his pack, but he was the first one to kill another human being, to kill a Russian.

As the members of his pack started ripping apart the dead Russian POW, which was when Heinrich came over, once again laughing and smiling. "Excellent, he didn't even have a chance! With a nose like yours maybe you will be able to track down escapees from the concentration camps." He patted Rudolph on the head. "But I think I have something better for you. With skills like that I think that you would be better on the Russian front. But I am getting ahead of myself, you still have much more training ahead of you."

Over the next several weeks and months, Rudolph and the members of his pack learned how to use their werewolf forms for combat against armed enemies. Soon they learned to survive in the woods for several days at a time on their own, completely in wolf form. Then they started taking out targeted enemies, POWs who had crude weapons. Finally after many long months of training against all sorts of situations that they might experience in military combat they were ready to graduate.

"This should be a very proud day for you boys," Heinrich said subtly wiping away a tear. "Even though you are barely even 15 years old you have already proven yourself combat ready. In your werewolf forms you are basically unstoppable killing machines for the greater glory of the third Reich. Adolf Hitler himself would be proud of you, and you all are a credit to the Aryan race. That is why today you graduate from being boys to being men. In a short time you will be assigned to the Russian front where you will be able to weather the cold and the elements better than some of our most senior soldiers."

Rudolph indeed felt proud. One of the caveats of the lycanthropy virus is that it had a much more devastating effect on adults. When an adult soldier was injected with the werewolf virus sometimes they would go completely insane or would be unable to transform back. By injecting it just as puberty begins the body is able to adapt to the transformation and it becomes much more natural. Once this was realized they began recruiting teenage boys for the werewolf experiments, and that was what was helping to turn the tide of the war in the favor of the Axis powers. The Allied powers of course wanted to learn the secret behind the werewolf soldiers, but so far that had proved elusive. But Rudolph wasn't worried, he felt a great sense of pride at the thought that he would soon be fighting for the Fatherland against the great hordes of Russians and other degenerates who were threatening the advancement of the German race.

Soon Rudolph and other members of his pack were recruited into a werewolf unit and stationed on the Russian front. Their task was to rampage across the frozen wasteland that was too cold and hostile for humans to navigate without being mowed down in large numbers.

"You go out there, and you go get them boys," a senior Nazi officer said as he and the boys did a salute as the boys began getting undressed and transforming into wolves.

Rudolph let out a loud howl signaling the rest of the group to follow him as they started charging across the frozen wasteland towards their Russian enemies.

The Russians of course opened fire on them, but the wolves were quick and extremely swift footed, and few of the bullets ended up hitting their targets. It was rumored that the Russians were now using silver bullets, which were devastating to werewolves. Just a couple of bullets would be enough to create a blood poisoning that could kill all of them. That is why they had to be extremely careful to avoid being hit.

The day started off strong, with Rudolph and his pack tearing down Russian soldier after Russian soldier before they even knew what hit them. As Rudolph disemboweled and dismembered soldier after soldier he was beginning to feel more and more alive with each passing moment. There was something about tearing a man apart with your bare teeth and claws that was so visceral and so primal that being a human in combat could never compare.

Rudolph even thought to himself that other soldiers of the Reich would never know the joy of being a wolf, of the feeling of brotherhood that comes with being part of a pack. Rudolph and his pack were virtually inseparable, both in wolf form and in human form. Not only was Rudolph a member of the so-called master race, but he felt he was a new form of life that transcended human beings altogether. Werewolves were the future, humans were just going to be the prey. Once the third Reich had conquered the world the inferior peoples of the world would simply be food for the wolves of Germany.

However as Rudolph and the other members of his pack continued on, the Russian artillery began firing more heavily upon them. A couple of members of his pack were hit with the silver bullets and let off the large yowls of pain before falling to the floor and convulsing, some transforming back into human beings, the ultimate indignity. If Rudolph was going to die he wanted to die as a wolf, not as a man.

As they continued advancing into the Russian front, more and more members of his pack soon started falling. Eventually even Kurt and Max had been felled by the Russian machine gun fire. Now Rudolph was angry and out for blood. He charged across the frozen ground, practically skidding across it. He dodged all of the Russian gunfire that was fired at him and dove on top of a Russian tank and dragged a soldier out of the top of the tank using his incisors and tearing him limb from limb.

That was when Rudolph saw it, he could smell it, the soldier that had killed his two best friends in the world. He was going to make that soldier pay come hell or high water. Dodging machine gun fire from every direction he managed to jump over the machine gun turret and begin ripping apart the Russian soldier that had killed the other members of his pack. As he tore into the Russian soldier he had never felt a greater feeling of exhilaration in his entire life. He felt on top of the world, like nothing could possibly bring him down.

That was when he heard it; it was a gunshot so nearby that he didn't even realize what had hit him. He felt it right in his back and he could immediately feel the poison going through his blood. He had been hit with a silver bullet and now he could feel himself rapidly dying as more and more bullets entered his body.

He started to feel like his body was transforming back into human, but he fought against it with every fiber of his being. No, even if he was pumped full of silver bullet poisoning he wasn't going to let himself die human. As one final bullet entered his throat he let out one final ear piercing howl that he hoped even the spirits of the dead members of his pack would be able to hear.

As the final bullet entered his skull, his last thought was that he died the way he lived, as a wolf.

He wouldn't have had it any other way.

<u>Author Notes</u>

I can remember exactly what inspired this idea. I saw this movie about the brutality of war called Come and See, which is about a young teenage boy who was sort of growing up in Eastern Europe during World War II, when all of the violence and ethnic cleansing took place there. Somehow I thought that that made a good setting for a coming-of-age story, and I had this idea of a story about a boy growing up in a time of war and violence and genocide, but also trying to experience the normal teenage things such as first love amid the backdrop of a war. Then I thought we would also have that complicated by the fact that the girl that he happens to be in love with just happens to be a deadly werewolf to further complicate things.

I think specifically I was thinking of having this awkward teen who is in love with a woman in the leading up to war and trying to deal with the fact that she seems to be a literal monster, and how that influences his feelings towards her, and how he tries to deal with that, meanwhile she is dealing with it in her own way and then the war just happens to bring them together so that they both confront this strange situation on their own in a way that likely wouldn't have happened if they were in peace times. The idea of becoming a werewolf also can serve as a metaphor for the strange feelings that puberty brings with it.

I thought the how and why of why she becomes a werewolf weren't really that important to the story, but just how being a werewolf sort of complicates their relationship, but also allows her to come into her own, basically reclaiming her power and fighting back against the forces of destruction around her by embracing her werewolf form more or less. And there's just something cool about the idea of a killer werewolf fighting Nazis in the woods during World War II, it's just a concept that I really liked a lot.

And this wasn't the first time that I sort of combined the setting of a werewolf story with the Holocaust and World War II. A particular subset of stories that I seem to really like is pairing supernatural evil and occurrences alongside human evil and brutality. So this wasn't my first Nazi Holocaust World War II werewolf story, as I had written at least two of them before that that I intend for publication in a collection of werewolf stories, but I thought that they would make good bonus stories to include with this novella, as they play upon similar themes of people surviving war and the Holocaust through supernatural means.

The first one about The Wolfman at Auschwitz was more of a survival story in the vein of this novella, where somebody uses the ability to turn into a werewolf as a way of fighting a back against the forces of evil trying to destroy them, with the werewolf ultimately becoming the lesser evil to fight against the more human evil of the Nazis and the Holocaust.

The second story, I Was a Werewolf in the Hitler Youth, is also somewhat similar to the themes of this novella but from the opposite perspective, where it's the Nazis who are turning children into literal monsters. I guess the story could also serve as sort of an analogy or a metaphor for just how children recruited into the Hitler youth were made more brutal, where in this case they just literally do you turn into vicious monsters, so it's really about the evil and corrupting aspects of fascism making monsters out of children. And there were actually was a Nazi fighting unit named werewolves I think, so I thought what about taking that to a more literal sense of the Nazis literally transforming children into werewolves for the purposes of war. There's something supremely evil about that which I think just works as a good way of showing how fascism corrupts and destroys our humanity.

I have no doubt that I will write many more future stories

both involving werewolves, World War II and the Holocaust and some combination of those things, but for now I think that these stories all serve as a good beginning and I hope that you enjoyed this and that it also made you think about how you don't have to be a literal monster to be a monster nonetheless, and that sometimes those who are literally monsters from our perspectives can actually be the good guys and the heroes, just trying to survive amid the worst possible circumstances.

Stephen Sipila

3/2/2022

Read excerpts from my books and stories in my blog at https://stephensipila.wordpress.com/ and follow me on twitter at https://twitter.com/StephenSipila